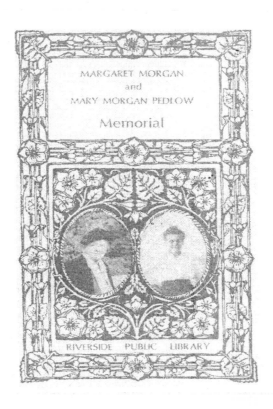

MARGARET MORGAN
and
MARY MORGAN PEDLOW

Memorial

RIVERSIDE PUBLIC LIBRARY

The
Problem
with the
Puddles

The Problem with the Puddles

(Pencil not required for reading, but may come in handy.)

WARNING: Writing or drawing in library books is bad for their health.

KATE FEIFFER

illustrated by
TRICIA TUSA

A PAULA WISEMAN BOOK

SIMON & SCHUSTER BOOKS FOR YOUNG READERS

New York   London   Toronto   Sydney

SIMON & SCHUSTER BOOKS FOR YOUNG READERS
An imprint of Simon & Schuster Children's Publishing Division
1230 Avenue of the Americas, New York, New York 10020
This book is a work of fiction. Any references to historical events, real
people, or real locales are used fictitiously. Other names, characters, places,
and incidents are products of the author's imagination, and any resemblance
to actual events or locales or persons, living or dead, is entirely coincidental.

Book design by Laurent Linn
The text for this book is set in Buccardi.
The illustrations for this book are rendered in pencil, crayon, and watercolor.
Manufactured in the United States of America
2 4 6 8 10 9 7 5 3 1

Library of Congress Cataloging-in-Publication Data
Feiffer, Kate.
The problem with the Puddles / Kate Feiffer ;
illustrated by Tricia Tusa.—1st ed.
p. cm.
"A Paula Wiseman book."
Summary: The Puddle parents cannot seem to agree about anything,
but when their dogs go missing the whole family embarks on an
unlikely quest that eventually answers many unasked questions.
ISBN: 978-1-4169-4961-9
[1. Dogs—Fiction. 2. Lost and found possessions—Fiction.
3. Family life—Fiction.] I. Tusa, Tricia, ill. II. Title.
PZ7.F33346Pr 2009 [Fic]—dc22 2008051388

For my dad, Jules, and for Jenny

—K. F.

To author Alice Miller

—T. T.

The
Problem
with the
Puddles

RAIN FALLS ON THE PUDDLES

Monday Morning, August 31

A cloud hovers over the Puddles.

Every day clouds zipped across the sky until they got to the Puddle property. No one knew why. All anyone knew was that when a cloud did get to the Puddles' house, it stopped. It took time out of its busy schedule to hang out for a while and practice its shape-making. It was as if the cloud suddenly forgot it was heading to a hurricane in Florida or an important blizzard in Canada. Perhaps it knew a family named Puddle lived below, or perhaps, as Baby Puddle believed, there was a big sign in the sky above their house that said STOP FOR PUDDLES.

On this particular morning on the last day of August, under a dog-shaped cloud, the Puddles dashed back and forth between their station wagon and the house. Baby Puddle loaded a backpack; a suitcase; three board games; her roller skates; her favorite stuffed dog, named Snore; and twelve cans of dog food into the car. Tom Puddle carried his backpack; a suitcase; his records; a record player; his oldest stuffed bear, named Bert; and a baseball bat out to the station wagon. Mr. Puddle returned to the house for "just one more thing" twenty-two times, and Mrs. Puddle crammed books into every empty space she could find.

At first the Puddles' two dogs traipsed behind, back and forth, from house to car to house to car to house to car to house to car. Then they wised up, sat down in the grass, and watched the people Puddles load up their Ford Country Squire.

The shiny red car with wood-paneled siding sunk down under the weight of so much stuff. Amazingly, the house didn't appear much emptier, even as the car filled all the way up. Boxes remained stacked on top of other boxes. Shopping bags, backpacks, and suitcases littered the hallway. The Puddles probably would have kept trying to jam things into the car, except that Mrs. Puddle looked at her watch and screeched, "Okay, guys, it's time to go. We're done.

We're packed. Let's get into the car. Scoot."

They looked at the car and could barely see through the windows. Baby wondered how they'd possibly all fit in it. Mrs. Puddle didn't really care how; she'd do whatever it took. Tom hadn't seen his best friend for two months, so he planned on holding his breath for the entire ride if he had to do that to fit in. Baby wanted to make sure she fit in because she missed her city bedroom, but since she was skinny, she figured she could fit anywhere. Mr. Puddle thought that if he didn't fit, he'd stay in the country, but his seat was the only empty one. Mrs. Puddle didn't like to drive on narrow curvy roads. She refused to drive more than thirty-five miles per hour, so she couldn't drive on the highway, and she positively hated driving onto the ferry. So Mr. Puddle generally sat in the driver's seat, which happened to be the only seat without something already on it. He sighed a deep, sad, long groaning sigh and got into the car.

Before Baby got in, she looked up at the sky and saw the dog-shaped cloud. It lifted its back leg. Sure enough, rain fell on the Puddles.

2

SUNDAY'S STORM

"Do you think it'll ever stop?" asked Baby.

"Sure it will," said Tom. "But it needs our help."

Tom walked into the middle of the room and started singing. Baby grabbed the orange tablecloth off the kitchen table and swung it into the air. Thunder that sounded like monsters clapping provided a most excellent drumbeat for a "stop the rain" song. Baby danced and Tom belted out all the rainy day songs he could think of. Mrs. Puddle joined in too. Fluorescent streaks of lightning added a dramatic touch to her operatic rendition of the "Rain, Rain, Go Away" song.

Mrs. Puddle couldn't wait to get back to the city. She told Baby and Tom she might lose her

4

mind if she had to stay in the country another day, and worried that if she lost her mind, she'd have a hard time finding it again. After singing her song, she plopped herself into a chair, placed her elbows on the kitchen table, and grasped the top of her head. Baby wondered if her mother were trying to hold her mind in place so it wouldn't get lost. Mrs. Puddle wanted to like the country. She wished she liked the country. But no matter how hard she wanted and no matter how much she wished, she didn't like the country.

The only good thing she could say about it was, "The country is nice on paper." Neither Baby nor Tom knew what she meant by that. All they knew was that she bellowed every time she saw a bug and shrieked whenever Charlie, the mouse that lived under the stove, ran through the kitchen.

Their dad felt entirely differently. Mr. Puddle loved the country and hated the city. Every year he'd say, "A country mouse like me can't possibly enjoy winter in the city."

He hoped the storm would never end.

Every few hours he'd sneak into the den to sing a "rain, rain, stay and stay, and whatever else you do, don't you dare go away" song.

The long rainy day kept the Puddles singing and dancing and wishing for the wind and rain to stop and wishing that the wind and rain wouldn't stop, depending on who was doing the wishing. The gray day eventually faded to the deep dark black of a starless night. Then the rain let up and the wind stopped whooshing.

"The songs worked. It stopped raining. Let's go see if the ferry is running," said Baby. "I'm ready."

"I'm more ready," said Tom.

"I'm the readiest," chimed in Mrs. Puddle. "Get your bags."

"Ready or not, we're not going anywhere," interrupted Mr. Puddle.

"We are going somewhere. Kids, get your—"
THUNDERCLAP.

"What, Mom?" asked Tom.

"I can't believe it," said Mrs. Puddle.

"Are the lights flickering, or is it me?" asked Baby.

"Naw, they're not flickering. They're out," said Tom.

"The electricity is out?" shouted Mrs. Puddle, without realizing that everyone could still hear her even if they couldn't see her.

"I'm afraid so," said a smiling Mr. Puddle. "Let's go to bed."

Mr. Puddle knew that in the dark no one could see his smile, so he smiled as broadly as his cheeks would allow. Mrs. Puddle knew no one could see her tears, so she let a few slip out of her eyes. And Charlie the mouse knew no one could see him run across the kitchen table, so he climbed up to collect some abandoned crumbs.

The Puddles stumbled and stubbed toes in search of their rooms. The wooden floor creaked with each step. Several bruises and bangs later, they found their beds, snuggled in, and went to sleep. No one knew on that rainy Sunday that the storm would last an entire week. That's the thing about day befores. Even if you think you know what's going to happen the next day, or the day after that, you never really know until it's happening. The Puddles figured the storm would probably be over on Monday, and the ferry would start running again by Tuesday at the latest. They certainly couldn't know how long the wind would keep whipping the trees and flicking shingles off the side of the house, and of course they had no idea about the events that would befall them on the day the storm finally ended.

THE STORM CONTINUES

The rain continued to make puddles. Baby, Tom, and Mrs. Puddle did their part to stop it. Mr. Puddle tried his best to keep the rain raining and the wind pounding just enough so that the ferry wouldn't be running and they couldn't leave the country. Sunday's storm turned into Monday's storm, which later merged with Tuesday's storm, which stuck around until Wednesday's storm took over. Thursday's storm brought enough wind to topple two trees, and the gusts grew for Friday's storm. By Saturday's storm, puddles looked more like ponds, and on Sunday, the storm was back where it had started an entire week before. After all, it was Sunday all over again.

Each day new clouds rolled in. Baby wondered if the clouds convened for a breakfast meeting each morning to decide on a theme for the day.

She noticed that:

Monday's clouds looked like dinosaurs.

Tuesday's clouds looked like hands.

Wednesday's clouds looked like polar bears.

Thursday's clouds looked like shoes.

Friday's clouds looked like sea horses.

Saturday's clouds looked like hats.

And Sunday's clouds looked like cats.

MRS. PUDDLE

Mrs. Puddle kept her eyes focused on the clouds. "Get out of here. Out of here. Out of here. O-U-T spells 'Out'! Out! Out!"

Mrs. Puddle spelled a lot of words. Sometimes she'd even say her punctuation out loud, like: "I'm going to the store now, exclamation point." Baby figured she did this because she was a writer who wasn't writing. If she'd been a writer who was writing, she could have spelled her words and used her punctuation on paper, but since she wasn't writing, she had nowhere to put her spelling and punctuation, so she put them in her talking.

Mrs. Puddle had published two books and then run out of ideas. Her first book was about the brother she never met. That's because six years before she was born her parents had a son whom they put up for adoption. "We were too young. We didn't think we would be able to take care of a baby. We wanted the baby to have parents who knew what to do," they told her. They said when she was born, "When you came, we were just the right age to have children." But after that they moaned, "We feel too old to have another child." So Mrs. Puddle grew up an only child, longing to meet the brother she never knew. Sometimes she wished so hard that her head ached and her back itched. When she grew up, she wrote her first book and dedicated it to her brother.

Every chapter in the book described what her brother might be like. In one chapter she imagined he was six feet tall and a professional baseball player with a long mustache that dangled off one side of his face. In another chapter he was small enough to fit into her hand.

Mrs. Puddle wrote her second book ten years later. *Agreeing to Disagree* became an instant bestseller, which meant the Puddles could have a house in the country under a cloud and an apartment in the city. It also meant the Puddles never agreed on anything.

AGREEING TO DISAGREE

If Baby's mom said yes, her dad said no. If her mom said, "You need to eat your vegetables," her dad would say, "It's time for dessert." Sometimes Baby thought that agreeing to disagree was the only thing her parents actually agreed on and that they had forgotten about the whole agreeing-for-the-sake-of-agreeing part of life. She sometimes wondered if her parents would have anything to talk about if they started agreeing on things. But since they didn't agree on much at all, they could talk forever and ever about everything they didn't agree on, and that was almost everything.

Baby's brother, Tom, claimed that their parents had agreed on everything in the world, and the state, country, and universe, until eight and a half years ago, when Baby was born. Tom said that if Baby had never been born, they'd still agree on everything.

But when Baby was born, that all changed

because they couldn't agree on what to name her. And after that they pretty much never agreed on anything else.

When Baby was born, Mrs. Puddle took one look at her adorable little face and knew her name should be Emily. But when Mr. Puddle looked at his daughter, he thought she looked exactly like his favorite aunt, Ferdinanda, so he wanted to name her Ferdinanda. Mrs. Puddle hated the name Ferdinanda. She said it was an unbelievably terribly bad name. Mr. Puddle said Ferdinanda sounded like the name of a sweet angel.

"Or a cow," said Mrs. Puddle.

"It doesn't matter," said Mr. Puddle, "because the baby looks nothing like an Emily and everything like Aunt Ferdinanda."

For the next day they went back and forth between the two names.

"Emily."

"Ferdinanda."

"Emily!"

"Ferdinanda!"

"Emily!!!!"

"Ferdinanda!!!!"

Other people jumped in to try to stop the fighting and suggested entirely different names.

"What about Halley?" asked Mrs. Puddle's best friend, Marcy.

"Her name is Emily. That's final," responded Mrs. Puddle.

"No, it's Ferdinanda," said Mr. Puddle.

"I like Rachel or Sarah," said Mrs. Puddle's mother. "They're classic names and very patriotic. Did you know that Paul Revere's wives were named Rachel and Sarah? You can't get much more American than Paul Revere or his wives or his horse, but I don't know his horse's name."

Mr. Puddle's mother said, "I want you to name her Juliet. My mother's name was Juliet, and this baby's name should be Juliet too. And anyway, my sister Ferdinanda does resemble a cow. Juliet here is beautiful and looks nothing like a cow."

"I like mysterious names. Call her Greer," said the lady sharing Mrs. Puddle's hospital room.

Tom Puddle knew he had come up with the best options of all. "Let's name her Goaway or Getoutahere."

"No! No! No!"

"Her name is Emily," insisted Mrs. Puddle.

"Ferdinanda," insisted Mr. Puddle.

When the time finally came to fill in the box that instructed "Write Baby's Name Here" on the birth certificate, Mr. Puddle took the pen and started to write "Ferdinanda." Mrs. Puddle reached across her hospital bed and grabbed the pen and paper out of her husband's hands and began to write "Emily." Mr. Puddle tried to get the pen back, but Mrs. Puddle pulled so hard that the pen flew across the room. A nurse picked it up off the hospital room floor, snatched the piece of paper out of their clutches, and wrote the word "Baby" in the box.

Baby was born eight and a half years ago, yet to this day Mrs. Puddle calls her daughter Emily and Mr. Puddle calls her Ferdinanda. Everyone else calls her by her real name—Baby.

THE BEST DISAGREEMENT

The best part of having parents that didn't agree was the presents. If Emily—that is, Ferdinanda—that is, if Baby wanted something special, she generally ended up getting two somethings—the special something she wanted and another slightly less special but still usually pretty cool something. Sometimes the whole present thing worked out so well for her that her friends said, "I wish my parents would stop agreeing." Or they'd say, "When my parents stopped agreeing on things, all I got was divorced parents."

Baby and Tom got their favorite presents over disagreements: dolls and bikes, electronic games and fancy books with moving parts. Often disagreements over what to eat for dinner, where to go for vacation, and where to live ended with more presents, extra vacations, and houses under clouds.

Baby and Tom agreed that one disagreement stood out as the best disagreement ever. The Puddles had wanted to get a dog. Naturally, Mr. and Mrs.

Puddle hadn't been able to agree on what kind of
dog. So they got two dogs, a tiny teacup Chihuahua
named Sally and a huge Great Dane named Sally.
Both dogs were named Sally because they couldn't
agree on which dog should be named Sally. Having
two dogs with the same name was confusing, but
Tom and Baby didn't care because they got a big
Sally and a little Sally instead of just one Sally. And
it really didn't matter anyway, because
whenever anyone called "Sally, come!"
usually only big Sally would come.

THE STORM ENDS, FINALLY

On Monday morning, a week and a day after that
old storm rolled in, Baby woke up to almost sunny
skies. All the clouds, aside from one dog-shaped
cloud, had taken off in pursuit of a new storm. Baby
ran through the house and pounced on her parents'
bed. "We can go! Get up!"

"What, Emily?" said a groggy Mrs. Puddle.

"Look out the window. Come on. Get up, Dad.
Get up."

"Do I have to, Ferdinanda?" asked Mr. Puddle.

"Yes! Yes! Yes!"

Mr. Puddle stretched his back and let his eyes
wander over to the window. "You might be right.
Let's turn on the television and check the weather
forecast." Mr. Puddle leaned over and turned on the
small black-and-white television set. *Please, John
Jakes,* he thought. *Give me another week of rain, just*

one more week. All I want is one more tiny little week of rain.

John Jakes, the weatherman on Channel 6, announced: "The rain's gone. The clouds have moved on. We've got sunshine everywhere you look."

John Jakes apparently had not looked at the Puddles' house, because if he had, he would have said, "The rain's gone and the clouds are gone except for at the Puddles', where there's a huge dog-shaped cloud."

The moment Mr. Puddle saw John Jakes's glistening white teeth, he knew his good luck had ended. They'd be heading back to the city. "Maybe we can stay here one more day?" Mr. Puddle asked wistfully.

"Not a chance," said Mrs. Puddle, who started humming her favorite Beatles tune before her feet hit the ground.

Baby tore through the house, yelling, "We can go. We can go. Tom, get up. We can go."

The two Sallys, who were sometimes referred to as Sally Squared, got caught up in all the excitement and barked a few times. They kept their eyes on the Puddles as they gathered their toys and bags, and ran along behind them for a while as they loaded up the car. When they got bored, they found a comfortable spot on the sidelines to watch the action. Big Sally rested her chin on her right paw, but little Sally kept her head raised.

The Puddles ran into the house, grabbed some bags, stuffed bags into the station wagon, ran back into the house, grabbed more bags, stuffed these bags into the station wagon, ran back to the house, grabbed even more bags, and so forth. The Sallys watched as Tom, Mr. Puddle, and Mrs. Puddle squeezed into the overstuffed car. They watched as Baby looked up and saw the dog-shaped cloud lift its leg, and they watched as Baby jumped into the car to avoid the rain. They kept watching as the Puddles drove off, leaving them in the rain under the dog-shaped cloud.

8

SALLY SQUARED

"They'll be back," said big Sally.

"I wonder," replied little Sally.

The two Sallys lay down next to each other and kept their eyes on the road.

THE DISCOVERY

Seventy-four miles into the trip Baby yelled, "Where's Sally?"

"Shhhh," scolded her mother. "You're being too loud."

"Where's Sally?" Baby screeched.

"Emily, I told you, not so loud."

"But, Mom, the Sallys aren't in the car."

"What?" queried Mrs. Puddle.

"Sally and Sally aren't in the car. Where are the Sallys?" cried Baby.

Tom yelled out, "Dad, stop the car. We forgot the Sallys."

Through her tears, which sprouted forth as though from a sprinkler, Baby said, "I can't—"

A big breath and more tears.

"—believe—"

Another big breath and still more tears.

"—we forgot Sally and—"

Then an explosion of tears turned Baby's sprinkler into a fire hose.

"—SALLYYYYYYYYYYYYYYY!"

"Emily." Mrs. Puddle turned around in her seat and put her left hand on Baby's knee. "Don't worry." She removed her hand, looked at her watch, and started calculating. Almost two hours into an eight-hour car ride meant that turning around made four hours into an eight-hour car ride without even beginning the eight-hour car ride.

8 - 2 = 6 hours. (Amount of time left before reaching the city if they didn't turn around.)

$$\begin{array}{r} 8 \\ -2 \\ \hline 6 \end{array}$$

2 + 2 = 4 hours. (Amount of time spent driving if they turned around and went back to the country.)

$2 + 2 = 4$

4 + 8 = 12 hours. (Amount of time spent driving if they went back to the country and then went to the city.)

$$\begin{array}{r} 4 \\ +8 \\ \hline 12 \end{array}$$

If this final equation happened, the car ride would last an intolerable

TWELVE HOURS.

However you do the math, twelve hours is a long, long time to be sitting in a car, especially a car that's so full there's barely room left for the oxygen you need to breathe. No, that couldn't happen. Mrs. Puddle couldn't stand the thought of a twelve-hour car ride, and anyway there was no room for the dogs in the car. But most of all she didn't want to go back to the country.

"When we get to the city, I'll call the neighbors and ask them to take care of the Sallys until we can get back, b-a-c-k, to the country and pick them up. You see, there's an easy solution and nothing to worry about."

"We can get back to the country in less than two hours," said Mr. Puddle. "No need to call anyone."

"Honey, I can't go back today." Mrs. Puddle spoke in a calm firm voice. She intentionally deleted all question mark sounds, so that no one could possibly think she wasn't entirely sure of what she wanted to do. Her tone didn't waver and her words fell out of her mouth with the same drive with which a hammer falls on a nail. "We need to go to the city. It's urgent! Just so you're not confused, I want to make sure you hear my exclamation point. We can call the neighbors. They will get the dogs, and you can go back to the country and pick them up later in the week, or over the weekend, or tomorrow, if you feel like it. I don't really care. I will not be able to accompany you. Whenever you go retrieve Sally Squared is fine with me, except for today. We are not returning to the country today. Let's keep going, g-o-i-n-g. I don't have the time for this. I'd like to get to the city before dinner."

"You don't have the time?" Mr. Puddle looked angry. The lines in his brow deepened and his lips clenched. "The time? The time! The time?!#!*#?! The time—"

Baby thought her father had gotten stuck on the word "time" and needed help moving forward, so she jumped in. "Dad, please can we go back?"

Mr. Puddle spoke slowly, so that each word floated out of his mouth and hovered in the air for a while before dissipating.

"Yes,

                   Ferdinanda.

          Now

    is

the

           time.

         We

             will

not

        abandon

                 those

       dogs."

       (Poof)

Mrs. Puddle decided to change her tone to light and cheery. "Don't be such a worrier. The dogs will be fine. They're so talented and competent." She figured everyone liked to agree with a cheery person.

Mr. Puddle had no cheer. All he had was a loud voice.

"The

           Sallys

                       need

                                  us."

Baby and Tom looked at each other. Parents that agreed to disagree could be a total drag. Sometimes nothing got done because Mr. and Mrs. Puddle spent so much of the day disagreeing. A typical day started with a disagreement over what to eat for breakfast and ended with a disagreement over what time Baby and Tom should go to bed. There might be a hundred disagreements in between those two disagreements.

Baby figured that by the time this particular disagreement ended, they would have driven for another hour, and then they'd have to start disagreeing all over again because they'd be almost three hours into the trip. She did the math, using her fingers, and it made her very nervous.

8 - 3 = 5 hours. (Amount of time left to drive before reaching the city if they didn't turn around.)

3 + 3 = 6 hours. (Amount of time they would be driving if they turned around and went back to the country.)

6 + 8 = 14 hours. (Amount of time spent driving if they went back to the country and then went to the city. And that didn't include however long it would take to find the dogs. Yikes.)

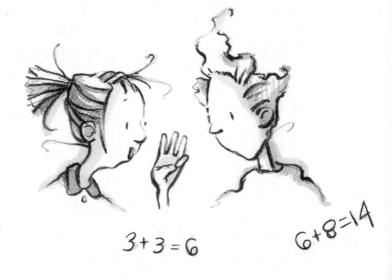

8-3=5

3+3=6

6+8=14

10

BACK AT THE PUDDLES' HOUSE IN THE COUNTRY

"Can I stand under you? It's raining," asked little Sally.

"Then I'll be wet and you'll be dry, and that's not fair," replied big Sally.

"Okay. You can stand under me," said little Sally.

"I don't fit under you."

"Well, why don't you try to fit," said little Sally.

"Okay," said big Sally, as she tried to slip, squeeze, and squish herself under little Sally. It should be noted here that a teacup Chihuahua isn't much bigger than a teacup of tea, and a Great Dane is larger than some small horses.

By the end of all her slipping, squeezing, and squishing, big Sally had successfully gotten her front right paw under little Sally.

"Are you dry?" asked little Sally.

"No. It's not working."

"Well, at least you tried. Do you think I should sit under you so at least one of us stays dry?" asked little Sally.

"I don't want to be the only wet dog here," replied big Sally. "Because then I'll smell bad and you'll still smell good and you'll complain that I smell bad."

"I promise I won't complain," said little Sally as she quietly stepped under big Sally and looked around for a comfortable spot to snuggle in.

"Why don't we go inside where we can both be dry?" asked big Sally.

"Because then we can't watch the road," said little Sally.

SIDEWAYS PUDDLES

He swerved left. Then he swerved right. Mr. Puddle was trying to decide what to do. When he thought *I should turn around immediately,* the car swerved left. When he thought *I'll wait to find a good safe place to turn around,* the car swerved right. For nine tenths of a mile the car swerved to the left and to the right and to the left and to the right.

At one mile, left won.

Mr. Puddle realized he could easily drive another thirty miles swerving to the left and to the right before finding a good safe place to turn around. He saw many okay places, but a good safe place meant a streetlight or intersection. Since he didn't see any other cars on the road, he decided turning immediately was fine.

He swerved left. He didn't plan to swerve left again. He planned to turn, but the swerve is the first part of a turn, and before he got to the part of the turn that would make it an official turn, Mrs. Puddle said, "You're making me carsick."

So he swerved right. He didn't mean to swerve right. It was just a reflex, like when your foot swings up after the doctor taps your knee. Since he didn't mean to swerve right, he re-swerved to the left to get back to his turn. This time he must have made one swerve too many. Whatever it was, the swerve never became a turn. The car just stopped mid-swerve.

"Why did you stop?" asked Baby.

"What's going on?" said Mrs. Puddle.

"Dad, I don't think the middle of the road is a safe place to stop," warned Tom.

Mr. Puddle stepped on the accelerator. The car gasped. Steam wafted out of the hood.

"The car overheated," said Mr. Puddle. "Trust me, it's nothing to worry about. When it cools

down, we'll be fine. I'll hop out and push the car to the side of the road."

Mrs. Puddle slid over to the driver's seat to steer, and buckled up, just to be safe. Mr. Puddle mustered all his strength and steadily pushed the car onto the side of the road, where there was a remarkably small yet unusually steep hill. Such a hill could only satisfy a sledding mouse; few others would even notice it. But perhaps because the station wagon was loaded with so many boxes, bags, and books, or perhaps because the station wagon was already feeling a little wobbly, it rolled down the itty-bitty hill until it lost its balance.

"Are we sideways?" asked Mrs. Puddle. "Yes, we're sideways," she said, answering her own question.

"Did the car tip over?" asked Tom.

"Are you guys okay?" asked Mrs. Puddle.

"I'm okay," said Baby.

"I'm fine, but Baby's squashing me," whined Tom. "Move over!"

"I'm trying," exclaimed Baby. "But I can't. Anyway, you're nice and soft."

"I'm not soft. I'm a boy. Boys aren't soft."

"Soft boys are soft. I guess that means that you're a soft boy."

"A soft boy who's going to punch you if you don't get off of me right now."

"Mom, Tom said he's going to punch me."

"She's squishing me and she called me soft. I'm not soft."

"Stop fighting, you two. Emily, don't call Tom soft. Tom, let Emily squish you for another few minutes until we get o-u-t." Mrs. Puddle gently stroked the car door, like it was a cat, until she found the handle.

Sideways, nothing feels quite right and Mrs. Puddle simply couldn't remember how to open a car door. Were you supposed to pull the handle toward you? Were you supposed to push it away from you? Who knew opening a car door could be so very complicated.

"Anyone remember how to open a car door?" she asked.

"I do," said Baby.

"I do," said Tom.

Just then the door flung open and in popped Mr.

Puddle's face. "You guys all okay in there? Let me help you out."

"I'm stuck," said Mrs. Puddle.

"Mom, your seat belt," said Baby.

"Oh, that's right." Mrs. Puddle blushed. She started fiddling with her seat belt. "Anyone remember how to take off a seat belt?"

BACK AT THE
PUDDLES' HOUSE

"I don't think they're coming back for us," said big Sally.

"This is a conundrum," added little Sally.

"A what?"

"A conundrum. You know, it's a conun and a drum, a conundrum. Just like meat loaf is like a loaf of meat, a conundrum is like a drum of conun," explained little Sally without explaining anything at all.

"I don't know what 'conun' is and I don't know what a drum of conun is either," said big Sally.

"It doesn't matter. What we have here is a conundrum, and we need to figure out what to do."

"Maybe we should try to find the city," suggested big Sally.

"I think it's very far away," said little Sally.

"At least this way we're not stuck in a car. I hate being stuck in a car. I always get cramps in my paws," said big Sally.

"What about the ferry? They only let dogs on leashes on the ferry. I don't know how we'd even get off the island. We can't walk across that huge watery ocean. We have to take the ferry, and they're not going to let two dogs that aren't on leashes onto the ferryboat. It's another conundrum."

"No it's not," said big Sally. "Let's go inside and get a couple of leashes."

"I didn't just mean leashes. A person has to be holding the leash. And anyway, how do you think we'd get our leashes on all by ourselves?"

"I don't know. I hadn't thought about that. Maybe we could pretend to be someone's dog."

"I got it. We can sneak onto the ferry." Little Sally's ears pricked up, and her tail wagged as she thought about the fun they'd have sneaking onto the cavernous old ferryboat that transported all the people and cars and dogs and cats from the country to the road that returned them to the city. "I love sneaking around. It's so fun when no one knows you're there and they have no idea that you're seeing and hearing and smelling everything they do. I think my idea is a perfect idea. Let's sneak onto the ferry."

Big Sally dropped her tail toward the ground. "I'm not very good at sneaking around. Usually everyone sees me."

"Yeah, I guess they probably would," commented little Sally. She looked behind big Sally's huge head at her massive body.

"Why don't we walk down to the ferry? Maybe we'll find a secret entrance," suggested big Sally.

Little Sally agreed that the only way to figure out how to get on the ferryboat was to scope it out in person. The two dogs set off down the road toward the wharf, leaving the dog-shaped cloud behind them.

Fifteen minutes later they were surrounded by grown-ups and children and cars and dogs and the sounds of honking and crying and yelling and barking and cheering as the ferry unloaded. People rushed about, picking up their bags and saying hello and kissing good-bye and putting down the bags and reloading the ferry. All the while, no one seemed to notice the Sallys didn't have their leashes on, and more important, no one seemed to notice that they didn't have their people with them.

"Are you sure you can't sneak on?" asked little Sally. "Can you try to make yourself look a little smaller?"

"I don't get smaller than this. Have you ever tried to make yourself look bigger?"

"Sure," said little Sally. "I'm actually quite good at it. I'm making myself bigger now, and I think I see something we should look more carefully at over there. Follow me." Big Sally obediently trailed behind little Sally.

"Oh, that's just a luggage cart," explained big Sally, when they came upon the luggage cart.

"No, it's not just a luggage cart. It's our ferry ticket. All we need to do is hop on and hide. If you curl up and make yourself look like a big black-and-white suitcase and I make myself look like a fancy tan handbag, I bet no one will even notice that there's furry luggage that smells good on the cart. Do you think you can make yourself look like a suitcase? I know you're not good at sneaking around, and I don't expect you're much good at hiding or turning into a suitcase either, but do you think you can try this one time? Just pretend you're really a suitcase, not a dog trying to look like a suitcase. Before you know it, you'll probably forget you're a dog and you'll start trying to pack yourself."

"I'm a very good hider," boasted big Sally. "I just don't sneak well."

Big Sally stepped onto the luggage cart; little Sally revved herself up for the Olympic medal-winning jump she'd need to get onto the cart. "Focus. Focus," she whispered to herself. She kept her eyes on the cart while the muscles in her back legs pushed her body off the ground, carried her through the air like a fairy, and gently deposited her on top of big Sally's big paw. The two dogs snuggled in behind the suitcases and shopping bags and golf clubs and a giant stuffed giraffe that had already been loaded on. They nudged a few items

little Sally?

big Sally

aside and tried to look as baglike as possible.

"Shhhh, don't say anything."

"You don't say anything."

"Shhhh, I said."

"You shush."

"I am shushed."

"No, you're shushing. You can't be shushing if you're shushed."

"Okay, I'll stop shushing."

"Shhhh!"

A few more packages and bags got tossed onto the luggage cart. By the time the cart got loaded onto the ferry, only the keenest of eyes would have noticed the two dogs. Luckily for the Sallys, there were no keen eyes around that day.

The ferry left the small island where the Puddles had a house under a cloud.

Twenty minutes later the boat docked on the mainland. The Sallys jumped off the cart and tore down a long narrow road.

PROBLEM

"Okay, which way to the city?" asked little Sally.

"It smells like it's this way. Let's walk in this direction," said big Sally.

The Sallys walked past a few houses and hundreds, maybe thousands, of trees. They found six lost tennis balls and a dead bird that didn't taste very good. The grass smelled like delicious fried chicken, and a few of the bushes they past smelled exactly like macaroni and cheese.

All was well, until all stopped being well. And all stopped being well when little Sally howled, "We have a big problem."

"We do? What's the problem?" asked big Sally.

"I'm tired. That's the problem. Exhausted. Out of steam. Unable to go on. That's the problem," said little Sally while sitting down next to a rock that was more than twice her size.

"That's not a big problem," said big Sally.

"But I'm really, really tired."

"I'm telling you that's still not a problem. That's a small problem, and a small problem is barely a problem at all," explained big Sally.

"Do you know how tired I am?" inquired little Sally.

"I think so, but why don't you tell me?"

"I'm sixty thousand steps tired. That's how tired I am. By my calculation, you're only six thousand steps tired. Which means that I'm ten times more tired than you are, and if you're even a little bit tired, multiply it by ten and you'll end up with a big problem."

Big Sally did the math.

```
  6,000
 x 10
 60,000
```

Little Sally's calculations were correct, but even so, big Sally still didn't see the problem.

Little Sally continued, "I sometimes wonder if

you think a small dog can even have big problems. I sometimes wonder if you think only big dogs have big problems and small dogs just have little trifling negative-number problems. But I'm telling you, I have a big problem."

"No problem. Just get up and keep walking. You'll be fine. Honestly, you'll work through your tiredness if you just keep going. Don't think about it and the problem will go away."

"No," said little Sally, "I won't."

"What?" Big Sally quickly swung her head around, as if she were trying to look into her ear to see if there was something in there that turned words like, "Good idea," into words like, "No, I won't."

"No, I'm not walking anymore. I'm stuck to my problem and it won't go away."

"Fine," said big Sally. "Then stop walking. I'm going to keep walking. And if you're not walking and I'm still walking, it means I'll be getting closer to the city and you'll stay at the same distance from the city, and I'll keep getting closer to the city and you'll keep staying the same distance from the city. Then after getting closer and closer, I'll be in the city, and you'll still be here, next to that rock, which is rather far away from the city. I hope you have fun next to the rock. I'm going to the city." Big Sally picked up her giant paws and loudly loped down the road.

Little Sally sat down next to the rock and watched as big Sally got smaller and smaller and smaller.

big rock

SALLY SINGLED

Little Sally walked around the rock. She lay down on the right side of the rock. But it was the wrong side of the rock for comfort, so she moved to the left side of the rock, which as it turned out, was also the wrong side of the rock for comfort.

She moved to the front of the rock. Then she walked around to the back of the rock. This rock, she decided, was a bad rock. She looked around to see if there were better rocks nearby.

While straining her neck to look for rocks, little Sally noticed something coming up the road. It moved fast. Perhaps whoever it was would slow down when they saw her to say "Hi" and recommend a good rock. Or perhaps they'd speed by and not even notice that a dog the size of a teacup was sitting uncomfortably next to a bad rock.

For a long while she couldn't make out who was in such a rush to get down the road. She watched the little white-and-black blob getting larger and larger and larger. The little white-and-black blob eventually turned into a big white-and-black dog that looked enough like big Sally to be big Sally.

"You're back. Did you realize my rock was bad and come back to help me find a better rock to rest by?" asked little Sally.

"No," said big Sally, "I didn't come back to look for rocks. I came back because I had a good idea."

SALLY RESQUARED

Big Sally slowly walked around little Sally.

"Why are you looking at me like that?" asked little Sally.

"Just thinking," said big Sally. "How much do you weigh?"

"I'm not sure you're supposed to ask questions like that. Aren't those types of questions rude?"

"That's for people. Dogs don't care about weight."

"Okay. Then, I'll tell you. I weigh two and a half pounds."

"Two and a half pounds? Two and a half pounds!" Big Sally flopped her paws against the ground and howled. "What kind of dog weighs two and a half pounds? I have bones that weigh more than two and a half pounds. There are birds that weigh more than two and a half pounds. I can't believe it, two and a half pounds."

"I shouldn't have said anything," snarled an annoyed little Sally.

"I'm sorry. You're right," agreed big Sally. "You shouldn't have said anything."

"Ruff," barked little Sally. She'd spent a lifetime as a small dog and it wasn't always easy. Small dogs get stepped on, tripped over, and kicked. Small dogs can't jump onto high couches or jump off of high beds. Staircases look like Mount Everest. And then there's the name-calling. Small dogs get called things like "teacup," "toy," and "cutie-pie." Little Sally particularly hated being called a teacup or a toy. Did she look like a teacup? Could you buy her at a toy store? No, she was a dog. A dog that ran and barked and played and cuddled and made sure that her owners didn't stay sad for very long. Teacups cracked, and hot water spilled and burned hands and people cried. Toys broke and got thrown away and people cried. There was no connection whatsoever. In fact, to make this point known, she bristled and growled whenever anyone referred to her as a teacup or a toy.

"Two and a half pounds is the perfect size for a best friend. I wouldn't have it any other way. If you were any bigger, I couldn't carry you, and you'd be stuck sitting by a bad rock for the rest of your life. Yes," mused big Sally, more to herself than to anyone else, "two and a half pounds is perfect."

"Did you say carry me?" asked little Sally.

"Yes, I think two and a half pounds is likely the perfect size for a dog riding on my back. One pound would be too light; you might bounce off. Anything more than five pounds would start feeling too heavy and would drag me down. You never want to feel dragged down. A big dog like me needs to stay alert."

"You want me to ride on your back?" asked little Sally.

"Sure," said big Sally. "You're tired. I'm not. You don't feel like walking anymore; I still want to walk. I've got a big back and it's not doing anything at the moment, so why not hop on and we can go to the city together?"

Wow, thought little Sally. She had once spent an afternoon riding on Tom's and Baby's backs but had never ridden on a dog's back before. Big Sally looked sleek and slippery. How would she stay up there?

Big Sally could see that little Sally looked a bit nervous, so she lay down and said, "Why don't you find a spot where you're comfortable and I won't get up until you're ready?"

Little Sally rubbed her paw along big Sally's left side to see if she could feel any rough patches. She walked around to examine big Sally's face. She inspected her long snout and peered up into her giant ears. *I could probably fit my entire body in one of those ears,* she thought.

"Can I climb up your face?" asked little Sally. "I think I'll have an easier time getting all the way up there if I can grab on to your nostrils and whiskers and eyelids and ears."

"Just be gentle. I need all those things."

Little Sally scrambled up onto big Sally's nose, wrapped her two front paws around big Sally's left ear, and felt her way across big Sally's neck with her back paws. She almost lost her footing but held on tightly and managed to pull herself up onto the top of big Sally's head.

"Are you ready?" asked big Sally as she lifted up her head.

"Wee!" squealed little Sally. She slid down big Sally's neck. She stretched her tiny body out as far as it would stretch across big Sally's withers. At first both dogs felt awkward. Big Sally assumed little Sally would just sit on top of her. That's the way she would have done it. She figured little Sally could stick a paw under big Sally's collar to keep her balance. But little Sally devised a position that she felt would ensure her a safer ride and lay down sideways across big Sally's back. Big Sally started walking.

"Are you scared?" asked big Sally.

"Not really."

"Then why are you shaking?"

"I'm not shaking."

"Yes, you are."

"No, I'm not."

"But I can feel you shaking," said big Sally.

"It's not me you're feeling. It must be something else," explained little Sally.

"You think so? I wonder what's shaking," said big Sally.

"I do too," said little Sally.

The Sallys resumed their journey to the city. They walked for a while in silence. Little Sally took in the sights from her new vantage point. The trees seemed smaller and the sky looked closer. After she got used to seeing the world from a big dog's point of view, they launched into their favorite conversation. A conversation so fun, they tended to have it over and over again. A conversation they never tired of. They called it "the perfect conversation." It had to do with Baby and Tom.

"What's your favorite thing to do with Baby?" asked big Sally.

"Snuggle in her lap. You?" replied little Sally.

"Snuggle in her lap. What else?" asked big Sally.

"I like it when she carries me around the house. You?" replied little Sally.

"I like to play ball with her. What about Tom?" asked big Sally.

"I like when he carries me around the house. You?" replied little Sally.

"I like it when he tries to carry me around the house. He'll try all sorts of different ways to pick me up. He's still never been able to get all four of my paws off the ground at the same time."

"I miss them," little Sally said, sighing.

"Me too."

"Do you think the city still smells like it's in this direction?" asked little Sally.

Big Sally stretched her neck out as high as it would go. She raised her nose to the sky and took a long slow sniff. She turned to the left and sniffed. She turned to the right and sniffed. She sniffed and sniffed and sniffed and sniffed and sniffed and sniffed. And then, by accident, she snorted, kind of like a pig.

16

BACK AT THE PUDDLES' CAR

Once they were all out of the car, the Puddles stood in a straight line by the side of the road. Raindrops bounced off the tops of their heads. They looked up the road. They looked down the road. The road looked empty.

"We need a tow truck," said Mrs. Puddle.

"We need to find a ride so we can get back to the Sallys," said Mr. Puddle.

"We need an umbrella," said Baby Puddle.

"We need lunch," said Tom Puddle.

They looked up the road again. They looked down the road again. More raindrops bounced off the tops of their heads.

"We need a tow truck," said Mrs. Puddle again.

"We need to find a ride so we can get back to the Sallys," said Mr. Puddle again.

"We need an umbrella," said Baby Puddle again.

"We need lunch," said Tom Puddle again.

They looked up the road again. Yes, you can fill in the blanks about what happened next.

They looked _____ the road again. More _____ bounced off the tops of their heads.

"We need a _____," said Mrs. Puddle again.

"We need to find a _____ _____," said Mr. Puddle again.

"We need an _____," said Baby Puddle again.

"We need _____," said Tom Puddle again.

60

BETWEEN ONE AND TEN

Three or four or five miles later the Sallys stopped to rest by the side of the road. Little Sally dismounted and stretched her twiglike legs. Big Sally arched her back and stretched out her long basketball-player-like legs. She put her nose to the ground and sniffed around. "Do you think we're getting close to the city?"

"Definitely," replied little Sally.

"How close do you think we are?" asked big Sally.

"By the smell of it, I'd say we're closer to it than we are farther from it. If the country is at one and the city is at ten, I think we're at about seven."

"I still smell the country. I don't get any sense of city. I think we're at four."

"Since I'm used to being closer to the ground, I can smell sidewalks before you," said little Sally. "I'm detecting a very faint sidewalk scent. Really, it's just a trace of sidewalk mixed with honeysuckle and oak trees and daisies, with a hint of pine and a slight waft of shellac. You wouldn't notice it unless your head were close to the ground a lot. It's an extremely sophisticated mix of smells. I'm not sure big dogs pick up on all the nuances. But you might because you have such an exceptional nose for a big dog."

Big Sally raised her head and put her exceptional nose up in the air. "Up here I smell trees. A little while ago I smelled some fog and a bunny that I thought about chasing, but I let it go because I didn't want you to fall off my back. Why do you think they put the country so far away from the city?"

"Must have been a mistake. Which do you think came first, the country or the city?"

"The city definitely came first," said big Sally in her most knowledgeable tone.

"You think?"

"Sure."

"How come?"

"Just look at it. It looks so much older than the country. Everything is gray and cracked. The country looks green and fresh. The city's older. I can remember the city from when I was a puppy. I think the country just came around a few years ago."

"Yeah, I think you're right," said little Sally. "I'm sleepy. Do you want to take a nap?"

"Sure," said big Sally.

The two dogs headed down a grassy hill away from the road and walked into the woods. They found a shady spot under a pine tree, snuggled up in a dog heap, and closed their eyes.

18

THE DANCING PUDDLES

The Puddles spotted a car coming toward them.

"Let's flag it down," said Baby.

"You better believe we're flagging it down, Emily," said Mrs. Puddle.

"Look, he's going in the direction of the country," said a pleased Mr. Puddle.

"He's almost here." Mrs. Puddle lowered her hands to her knees and then, in a large swooping motion, lifted her arms above her head and skipped into the road. Like a swan about to take flight, she flapped her arms while she dashed up and down the wet road.

Baby Puddle leapt through the air with her arms stretched high above her head and her hands waving. Tom Puddle shifted from side to side, while thrusting both arms out diagonally in front of him. Mr. Puddle extended and then retracted his right arm repeatedly.

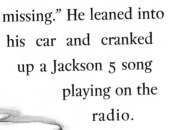

A light blue Volkswagen Bug approached quickly and then just as quickly screeched to a stop. A short man with dark brown hair, green pants, and a purple checked shirt popped out. "Bravo. Fantastic. Unbelievable," said the man, applauding. "What a show. But one thing is missing." He leaned into his car and cranked up a Jackson 5 song playing on the radio.

"Now try it to this music, and do tell me, do you perform elsewhere? Are you a real family like the Jackson Five or are you keeping that information a secret? Of course, the world loves a family that performs together. The world. The world. What a large mysterious place the world is. It is good. It is bad. It is full of happiness, sadness, and otherness. Sometimes real families perform together. Sometimes we bring people together for their art and call them a family. What is a family, really? And tell me what kind of family are you? You must tell me. No, don't tell me. That's private information. You mustn't. Oh, fine, I need to know. Are you a real family?"

Before any of the Puddles could say anything, the man continued on. "Performing by the side of a road. How brilliant. How magnificent. How groovy. Oh, tell me, please. You must. No, no, you must not. I need to know. I don't want to know."

"Excuse me, sir—" Tom tried speaking, without success.

"What do you call yourselves?" interrupted the man.

"We're the Puddles," replied Mr. Puddle. "And who are you?"

"Puddles. The Puddles. The dancing Puddles," said the man. He stretched himself out by standing on his tiptoes and ducked in, darted out, and sashayed through Baby, Tom, and Mr. and Mrs. Puddle. "Look at me. I'm prancing around the Puddles."

"We need a tow truck," said Baby.

"We need to get our dogs," added Tom. "We forgot them."

"Yes, we left them in the country," explained Baby.

"I see," said the man, who for the first time noticed that their car didn't have its wheels on the pavement. "I can help you. I can and I will help you. I shall help you. I'll even promise to help you. Okay, fine. I'll vow to help you. It is you that I will help. But first," said the man, "you must come back to my house and dance for my wife and have some lunch."

"We can't do that," said Mrs. Puddle.

"Sure we can," said Mr. Puddle. "It's the only available option."

"I'm afraid we'll have to w-a-i-t for another option to make itself available," responded Mrs. Puddle to her husband.

"No, we'll take advantage of this offer," responded Mr. Puddle to Mrs. Puddle's response.

Tom and Baby groaned. They knew their parents would spend the next fifteen minutes disagreeing over whether or not they should go to the man in the VW Bug's house and dance for his wife so they could get their car towed and get the Sallys. That is, if they could even agree on whether to get the Sallys now or later.

"Stop!" said the man. "You argue. You don't agree. You disagree. You won't agree. Can you agree? Should you agree? Have you agreed to disagree? You must come now, before immediately, and sooner than at once. I have a book for you. I call it *Agreeing to Disagree*. The author of the book also titled it *Agreeing to Disagree*. It's a wonderful coincidence. Don't you love wonderful coincidences? Now come and dance for my wife. I will give you the book. I will help you get a tow truck. I will get your dogs."

"That sounds like a wonderful idea," said a suddenly agreeable Mrs. Puddle, who made her way over to the Bug. "I look forward to meeting your lovely wife and seeing the other interesting books that you and your wife like to r-e-a-d."

She opened the passenger-side door, sat down in the front seat of the car, buckled herself in, and slammed the door closed. Since the only other door to the car was the driver's door, Baby opened the door that her mother had just closed, climbed over her mother, and plopped herself down in the backseat. Then Tom crawled over Mrs. Puddle into the backseat. Mr. Puddle noticed that the tiny backseat already looked cramped with just Tom and Baby sitting in it. He took a deep breath and shimmied into the car.

"You're sitting on me," said Mrs. Puddle.

"I know," replied Mr. Puddle.

"Why are you sitting on me?" asked Mrs. Puddle.

"Because you're in my seat," answered Mr. Puddle.

"Marvelous. We fit," said the man from the Bug. He placed his foot on the accelerator and pushed down. The car jolted forward and bucked a few times before hitting a comfortable driving speed. "Call me Frankolin, like violin, but say 'Frank' instead of 'vi.' Then use the same 'olin.' Yes, sometimes I think I'd be better off changing my name to Olin. It gets rather confusing. Once, I asked someone if they could play the violin, like Frankolin, and they said, 'You want me to play the violin like you?' And I said, 'No, not like me. I just want you to play the violin like Frankolin.'"

Frankolin told the Puddles he lived seven minutes away, and in fact, exactly seven minutes later they pulled up in front of a large pink and purple house. Frankolin's wife, a tall snarly-haired woman, came bounding out the front door.

"Felicia," he said, "I'd like you to meet the Puddles. They are a dancing troupe, and while they prefer to perform by the side of the road, I have convinced them to come dance for you. You see, their car had a bit of trouble. The wheels disconnected, disassociated, and distanced themselves from the road. They must reclaim their dogs, which they mistakenly left behind, and I have promised to help them as long as they dance."

"Fantastic," exclaimed Felicia. "Allow me to get the king." Felicia's long legs carried her quickly to the house. Baby had never seen such lanky legs before and wondered if they ever got tangled. When Felicia returned, she was carrying a reddish-brown and white dog. "May I have the honor of introducing you to the king. He's a Cavalier King Charles spaniel. We think that Staffordshire bull terriers invaded his kingdom and he had to flee. We found him limping along on the outskirts of Oaks Bluff. Dance performances remind him of the days when the Irish setters set things up in the grand ballroom for the terrier twist and the beagle ballet. Now tell me, where shall we sit? I do hope the driveway will suffice for a road."

The king barked three times and then sat down quietly.

The Puddles stood in a perfectly straight row.

They knew they were supposed to dance, but they weren't at all sure what kind of dance to do. After all, they weren't really a dance troupe that danced by the side of the road. They were just a normal family. Baby turned her head to look at Tom. Tom turned his head to look at Mrs. Puddle.

Mrs. Puddle turned her head to look at Mr. Puddle, and Mr. Puddle turned his head to look at Baby, who looked at Tom, who looked at Mrs. Puddle, who looked at—well, once again you can fill in the blanks. But actually, this time, you can't, because there are no blanks to fill in. Wait until next time.

The looking at one another continued until Baby diverted her eyes away from Tom and toward the sky. Tom noticed Baby look up, and he looked up. Mrs. Puddle noticed Tom look up, and she looked up. Mr. Puddle noticed Mrs. Puddle look up, and he looked up. A face-shaped cloud pointed down at them. Rain dribbled out of the nostrils.

"He has the sniffles," said Baby, sighing.

Baby didn't feel like getting wet again and dashed off in the direction of the house. Tom thought he should stop her, so he hopped up on his toes and lunged at her. Mrs. Puddle stretched out her arm to grab Tom and missed. Mr. Puddle ran to catch Baby, but twisted his ankle, fell to the ground, rolled around, and started howling.

"Isn't it wonderful?" said Frankolin. "They have such an unusual style. Such genius! Don't you think so, Felicia?"

"Why, yes," cooed Felicia in a gravelly voice. "I think they look like they're doing the mastiff mambo. Don't you, darling King?

The king looked into Felicia's eyes and barked.

LIKE DOGS

"Hey, Sally, wake up. We should get going."

Big Sally opened one eye. Everything looked blurry. She opened the other eye to clear things up, but everything looked wrong. Where was she?

"Huh?" grunted big Sally.

"I think we should keep walking. We want to make it to the city by nighttime."

Big Sally now remembered that she and little Sally had left home to find the rest of their family. She remembered that they had walked for a long time and decided to take a nap. It all came back to her. Even the smell of the pine tree seemed familiar.

"Why do you think they left without us?" she asked.

"I guess they forgot us," said little Sally.

"How come they forgot us?"

"I don't know. I wouldn't forget us. But they have more to remember, and humans forget a lot

74

of things because they're trying to remember so much."

"Do you think after a while your memory gets full?"

"Not mine. I remember everything."

"It's too bad humans aren't more like dogs," said big Sally.

"I sometimes think they act like dogs," remarked little Sally. "Sometimes Baby will do something  that reminds me of a dog. Sometimes I look at her and I think she's the cutest pug in the world. She has the perfect pug personality. She is happy so much of the time that it sometimes makes her grunt, and she always wants to play and snuggle. I think she's probably mostly human but part pug. Have you ever noticed that she likes to have her neck scratched and pulled? How pug is that?"

"I know what you mean," said big Sally. "I kind of think Tom acts like a chocolate Lab. Don't you?"

"Totally, or when he plays catch, he's such a

Lab–Portuguese water dog mix. Can you believe how high he can jump? No just-human boy can jump that high. What about Mrs. Puddle?"

"Come on. She's a Lhasa apso if I ever met one."

"I know it! The way she sometimes snarls for no reason at all is so Lhasa."

"Yes, and the way she'll play only when she wants to play and never lets anyone else start the game."

"What about Mr. Puddle? Don't you look into his eyes and think, this guy's a rescue dog?"

"Yeah, he's a mutt. Never has a bad word to say, nonjudgmental. He's the best kind of mutt. The kind of mutt my mother always told me to be friends with."

"Did you ever think you'd end up being best friends with a Chihuahua?" asked little Sally.

"Never. I never paid any attention to little dogs until I met you. I never even knew little dogs were real dogs until I moved in with the Puddles. I'm really glad they knew that big dogs and little dogs can be best friends. Sometimes humans can be pretty smart. It's just too bad their memories get so full."

The two Sallys got up from under the pine tree, shook themselves off, and walked back to the road.

BACK WITH THE PUDDLES
AT FRANKOLIN'S HOUSE

Frankolin's wife, Felicia, scratched the top of her head. She thought it would feel good to run her finger through her wild gray locks. Her unusually long pointer finger began navigating a course across the curls and through the ringlets, but crashed into a giant snarl before long.

"Oh, dear," Felicia mumbled. "Oh, well. Oh, my. Well, please do come inside. I apologize in advance for the mess. I'll get you some lunch."

"Don't worry about the mess," said Baby. "I love messes."

"Yes," said Mrs. Puddle to Frankolin and Felicia, "Emily really does love a good mess."

Felicia opened the door and kicked a coat from one side of the floor to the other. "Oh, my. I'm so sorry."

"Wow," said Baby. "You guys are like professional mess makers."

"Ferdinanda, shhh!" snapped Mr. Puddle.

Piles of papers, heaps of clothing, mountains of bottles, drifts of dust, and dozens of destroyed dog toys filled what looked like it once could have passed for a living room. A bookshelf was lined with books facing the wrong way. For years nobody had been able to tell what books were in it because the spines faced in and the pages faced out.

Mrs. Puddle tried to ignore the mounds of rubbish underfoot, and she did, except for one "Yuck" that escaped.

"Felicia, do you think I can use your phone to call our neighbors? I'd like them to check on our d-o-g-s."

"Of course. Just follow me. Step this way. There's a bit of a path here. Try climbing over this pile of clothing, if you don't mind. Don't worry. You won't hurt anything. It's just laundry. The funny thing is I forgot if the pile was clean or dirty, so I decided to put all our clothes in it. I figured it takes so much time to separate the clean clothes from the dirty ones, why not just keep them all together? We should be able to find a phone in the kitchen. They keep disappearing. I don't know where they go. They just never seem to stay in the same place."

Mrs. Puddle and Felicia stepped over and on candy wrappers, magazines, mismatched socks, a deflated balloon, a stuffed bear, a piece of wood, a frying pan, a tennis racket, two coats, a green shoe, a lamp, a wing from a model airplane, a photograph of a young boy, and a dog bone before reaching the door to the kitchen.

They pushed on the door, which was barricaded on the other side by pots and pans and plates and bowls and boxes of spaghetti and cans of soup. They nudged the door open enough to get through and slipped into the kitchen.

Fifteen or so minutes later Baby whispered to Tom, "Do you think we'll ever see Mom again?"

Tom whispered back, "I think we should go in after her."

Mr. Puddle shushed them.

"Dad, I'm really worried."

"Your mother is fine."

"Dad," said Baby, "we've already lost our dogs. I really don't want to lose Mom, too."

"I told you," said Mr. Puddle. "Shhhh."

A large crash rang out from behind the kitchen door.

"Mom?" yelled Baby. "Are you okay?"

BAD NEWS

Mrs. Puddle burst through the door.

"What's wrong?" asked Baby. "What was that noise? Why do you look so upset?"

"Oh, some pots and pans fell off the counter. The floor will hardly notice a bit more clutter. I'm fine. And I'm sure everything is fine. It's just that there is a little bit of bad news. I don't want anyone to worry. Let's take a d-e-e-p breath, comma, and relax. I'm going to say something that might sound scary, but it's not. It's fine. So I don't want you to feel scared even though you might want to feel scared. Don't worry. Everything is going to be okay, except there's one little problem. The neighbors can't find the Sallys. They walked around the house and searched inside. They said the place looked as empty as a fifth-grade classroom during winter vacation. Ha-ha, isn't that funny? I mean, not that the dogs are missing, but that they said the house looked as empty as a fifth-grade classroom during winter vacation. You get it? No one is there. Just like—"

"What?" interrupted Baby. "They're gone?"

"The dogs seem to be momentarily missing, Emily. May I emphasize the word 'momentarily.' Do you know what that means? It means they will show up soon, as in a few moments. The neighbors couldn't find them right now. But don't worry. The neighbors probably have bad eyesight. I think they wear glasses. I'm sure the dogs will turn up. They're on an island, after all. They can't go too far. And I also have good news. Yes, I do. I called a mechanic. He'll be towing the car to a garage to fix it, and soon enough we can get back on the road. If we're lucky, we'll get to the city before nightfall. Isn't that wonderful?"

"No, it's not. I can't find the good news here. Furthermore, we can't go to the city. We have to look for the Sallys," said Mr. Puddle. "I'm not just saying that because I want to go back to the country. I'm saying it because we need to find the dogs."

"No, we actually don't," countered Mrs. Puddle. "The Sallys will be fine. They'll go home. The neighbors will call when they do."

Baby and Tom knew this disagreement could take a while. Baby's eyes reddened.

Tom chewed on his bottom lip. "Come on, guys. We gotta get the dogs," he said.

Frankolin nodded. He bent down and reached under the couch until he pulled out two bars of soap. He placed them on the floor and stepped on them, like one might step on a stool. Then bellowed in a startlingly loud voice:

"Hear ye! Hear ye! We've received some troubling news. Two dogs have gone missing. I'm here to say, do not worry. Do not fret. The king will help us. He'll declare a proclamation. He'll proclamate a declaration. He'll announce a constitution and constitute an annunciation and a renunciation, along with an excavation. And then he'll launch an internal investigation."

Baby and Tom looked at each other. Baby twitched her nose to signal that they needed to take control of a bad situation. Tom nodded to say he agreed. Baby shrugged her shoulders to indicate she didn't have any ideas about what to do next. A tear dropped out of her left eye. Frankolin's wife, Felicia, looked lovingly at the king.

Tom coughed in an attempt to interrupt Frankolin, who by this point had gone on to discuss an event that occurred four score and seven years ago, which he claimed was the best year of his life, even though he hadn't been born yet.

"Excuse me, sir," said Tom. "I think perhaps if you would be so kind as to lend us—if we could borrow— Can we use your car while ours is getting fixed so we can try to find our dogs? If that's—"

Mr. Puddle interrupted his son. "We don't want to put you out, but it seems that we have an emergency."

"No, no, no," said Mrs. Puddle. "Our car is getting fixed. If Frankolin and Felicia don't mind, we'll stay here and wait for the mechanic to call. Then when our car is fixed, we'll drive to the city like we planned and figure out what to do with the dogs. Case closed. Period."

The king looked up at Mrs. Puddle. His nostrils quivered.

"Please, sit down," said Frankolin.

The Puddles looked around for any clear surface to sit on. There was none, so they sat on the mess.

"No, not you," said Frankolin. "I'm talking to the

king. Now talk to me so we can figure out what to do."

"Frankolin," started Mr. Puddle, "my son is right. Perhaps you'd be so kind as to lend us your car."

"No, not you," said Frankolin. "I'm talking to the king."

The king looked into Frankolin's eyes and barked.

THE SWIM

"Look. There's a river," said big Sally.

Little Sally had already noticed the river running parallel to the road but hadn't thought much about it since she wasn't particularly thirsty. The water looked like it tasted good, but not good enough to make a special trip.

"I'd like to take a swim. I'm kind of hot," said big Sally. "Do you want to go swimming?"

"No, not really," replied little Sally.

"Really?"

"I said *not* really," clarified little Sally.

"I know. I meant really not really when I said really."

"Yes, really not really, really."

"But I want to take a swim and I'm doing the walking, so if I take a swim, you'll have to come with me."

"I'll watch."

"From up there?" asked big Sally.

"No. I'll get down."

"I think you should swim."

"I don't want to."

"Why not?"

"Because I'm not too hot. I'm perfect hot, and swimming would make me not hot enough, but you should swim and I should watch to make sure you're okay."

"Good plan," said big Sally.

Big Sally turned and stepped carefully. She descended down a steep hill. Little Sally held on extra tightly as the ride got significantly bumpier. It's true that at first big Sally tried to walk as gently as possible, but the closer she got to the water, the more excited she got.

Little Sally held on for dear life.

When they reached the river, big Sally barely had the wherewithal to stop and let little Sally off her back. "Jump off quickly."

"Lie down so I can slide off."

"Okay, okay, but hurry. I don't know how long I can wait. That water is calling my name. Do you hear it?"

"No, frankly, I don't. All I hear is a gurgled waterflowy sound. It doesn't sound anything like 'Sally.'"

Little Sally slid off big Sally onto the pebbly shore. Big Sally charged into the water and started swimming. She chomped on a special stick that floated by and tossed it into the air. The water rippled around it when it landed. She swam through the ripples, trying to catch them in her mouth.

She flipped the stick back into the air. Both dogs watched to see where it would land. It didn't land. They looked up. Some overly leafy branches in a tree had captured big Sally's special stick. "My stick is stuck," moaned big Sally.

Little Sally watched from the shore and laughed.

After not a long time big Sally got bored of looking at her stuck stick. The stick started to look less like her special stick and more like all the other sticks. Soon she wasn't even sure if the stick she was looking at was even her stick. She swam to shore. "Do you want to watch me dive?" she asked.

"Can you really dive?"

"Sure. Watch this." Big Sally dropped under the water. When she came up for air, she saw little Sally bouncing up and down.

"That looked cool."

"Do you want to try?" asked big Sally.

"I don't know. I do, but I don't. I'm scared to swim. I think I better keep watching."

"But I'll help you and make sure you're okay," said big Sally.

"I think I'll just watch. I'm a good watcher and you're putting on a great show. If I come in, there'll be no one to watch your show, so I better stay here to do the watching."

"I don't need anybody to watch my show," said

big Sally. "It would be more fun to do a show with you and not have anyone watching."

"I'm too scared," said little Sally.

"Just try. Start by putting one paw in the water and see how that feels. If it feels good, put your other three paws in. If that feels good, take a few steps and you'll be swimming. If it doesn't feel good, you can get out."

"I don't know. I'm not a very good swimmer."

"Have you ever tried swimming?" asked big Sally.

"No, but I know I'm not very good at it. I can tell."

"I'll be right here if you need help, and I'm an excellent swimmer, lifeguard certified."

Little Sally walked to the water's edge and watched the gentle waves lap up against the shore. She stretched her neck out over the water to see if she could find her reflection, but the water was too busy to reflect for her.

"I still don't know," she said. "Maybe another time."

"If you want," said big Sally. "But it's really fun and I think you should try it this time."

Little Sally carefully placed one paw into the water. "It's not too cold."

"It's the perfect temperature," agreed big Sally.

Little Sally scooted up a tad more.

"How's that?" asked big Sally.

"It's great," said little Sally. She looked down and found her reflection.

"Do you want to swim?" asked big Sally. "I can teach you how to do the dog paddle. It's a very easy stroke, especially for a dog. All you need to do is lift up your paws and think about running."

Little Sally took a few more steps into the water. When her paws could no longer feel the ground below her, they started spinning around. "Look, I'm doing it," she squealed in delight.

"Isn't it easy?" asked big Sally.

"I know how to swim. I can't believe it; I know how to swim. Look at me."

"See if you can swim all the way to me." Big Sally moved a few dog lengths away from shore.

Little Sally's big eyes widened and she put her paws in motion, splashing and swimming and, then, reaching big Sally.

"Want a ride?" asked big Sally. She did a dog dive

and swam underwater until she reached little Sally.

Little Sally grabbed big Sally's collar when she surfaced and started pawing her way up big Sally's neck, which was as sleek as a sheet of ice. She had almost reached the top of big Sally's head when she slipped. She slid down big Sally's neck, across the length of her back, past her tail, out over the river, and down under the water.

Seconds passed. Minutes maybe? An hour? No sign of little Sally under the water. Big Sally started to wonder if her little friend had drowned. What felt like an hour had only actually been ten seconds. On the eleventh second, little Sally popped her head out of the water and exclaimed, "That was fun! Let's do it again."

Over the next fifty-two minutes little Sally discovered different methods of doing the Sally slide. She zoomed down headfirst. She zipped into the water tail first. She made loud splashes and you-can-barely-hear-them splashes. She tried to make her splashes sound like *faloush, shweethud,* and *flump.* Finally she got tired.

"Maybe we should walk again."

"Good idea," said big Sally. "Hop on. We still have a long way to go before we get to the city."

The dogs shook the water off their coats and climbed up the hill.

"The city is this way." Big Sally swung her nose to the left, and the two dogs set off to find the Puddles in the city.

BABY MAKES A MOVE

Baby looked around. She had once said she loved messy rooms more than chocolate, but chocolate was better than this mess. She made a mental note to not let her room get too messy. Too messy is bad messy. A mess needs structure.

Her father's face hung low like someone had sucked the air out of him. The circles under her mother's eyes seemed to be growing darker by the minute. Tom's hands turned into fists. Baby wanted her dogs. She wanted them so much that she knew she had to take action, and she finally figured out just what to do.

"Excuse me. Can I use the bathroom?" asked Baby. She had seen this trick done a thousand times on TV. You go to the bathroom and crawl out the window. By the time anyone figures out you're missing, you've already done all the things you need to do.

"Why don't you come with me," said Felicia.

The climbing over the mounds of rubbish began. Baby stepped on a lollipop that got stuck to the bottom of her shoe. Then she came upon a pile of towels that smelled like rotten milk, only worse. "Do I have to touch those?" she asked.

"Just try to jump over them," instructed Felicia.

No more messy room for me, ever, thought Baby as she jumped over the stinky pile.

Felicia led her out of the room and down a dark hallway. The walls were lined with children's paintings. A few golf clubs and paper plates rested on a rug.

"The bathroom is right here." Felicia pointed at a door with the word "Relief" painted on it.

"Thank you," Baby said as she opened the door. She stepped inside and saw pretty much the grossest sight she'd ever seen. It's not worth describing because it's too disgusting, but you can use your imagination. Better yet, don't even try to imagine it.

Then she spotted the window. Oh, beautiful window. Baby closed the door behind her, and looked out the window at Frankolin and Felicia's backyard. It didn't look like it had been mowed all summer. It didn't look like it had been mowed ever. Baby opened the window and crawled through.

LITTLE SALLY'S QUESTION

"I have a question," said little Sally.

"That's fantastic," said big Sally.

"Why is that fantastic?" asked little Sally.

"Because I have an answer."

"How do you know you have an answer when I haven't asked my question yet?" inquired little Sally.

"I know I have an answer because I have that answer feeling. I can feel things like answers before they come on. I feel a tingling when the phone is about to ring. I get a sloppy uncontrollably droolly feeling when my dinner is about to be served. My fur twitches when Baby and Tom are about to play with me. And I feel a ringing in my ear when someone's about to ask a question that I have the answer to. Right now the ringing is very loud. In fact, I can barely hear you."

"Okay. Then I'll ask my question," said little Sally. "Other than Great Danes and Chihuahuas, what's your favorite kind of dog?"

"What's that you ask? A little louder, please," said big Sally in a too loud voice.

"Other than Great Danes and Chihuahuas, what's your favorite kind of dog?" yelled little Sally.

"Is that your question?" big Sally yelled back.

"Yes."

"What?"

"YES."

"Hmmmm," murmured big Sally. "I don't know."

"What do you mean you don't know. You just told me you had an answer," said an astonished little Sally.

"You asked the wrong question. If you had asked the right question, I would have had an answer."

Now little Sally was having a hard time hearing, or at least believing what she was hearing. "So you're telling me you only had an answer to one question. What are the chances that I'd ask the one question you had the answer to? There are more than twelve trillion questions in the world. I myself have a trove of thirty-five questions at any given time. Don't you think it was misleading to say that you had an answer? I think you should have said 'I have one answer. If you don't ask the question to my answer, I won't have an answer.' That's what you should have said."

"But that would have been a lie. I have more than one answer. I had figured you'd ask a closed question. But you asked an open question. My ears were ringing for a closed question."

"What in the dog world are you talking about?" fumed little Sally. "Since when is a question open or closed? A question is a question. It wants an answer, just like a leash wants a collar. There are no such things as open or closed questions; there are simply questions. And you still haven't answered me. What's your favorite kind of dog?"

"Big or little?" asked big Sally.

"Either," replied little Sally.

"Herding or hound?" asked big Sally.

"Either," replied little Sally.

"Well," said big Sally, "to be perfectly honest, I like mutts. My favorite mix is one part golden retriever, three parts Australian shepherd, one and a quarter parts yellow Lab, one and a half parts pug, four parts beagle, a splash of Portuguese water dog, and a hair of poodle. So if you really want to know, that's my favorite kind of dog, other than Great Danes and Chihuahuas, of course."

"Wow, that's amazing," said little Sally.

"Really? Why?" asked big Sally.

"Because that's my favorite kind of dog too, other than Great Danes and Chihuahuas, of course."

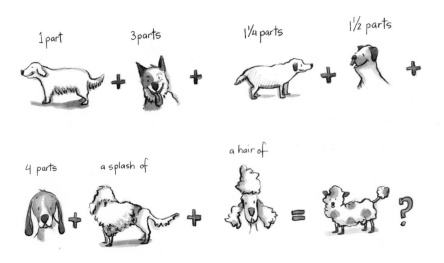

25

BABY ON THE MOVE

Baby looked around to make sure no one could see her and dashed down the driveway. When she reached the main road, she figured that she'd walk for a while to clear her head. All that mess had made her thoughts go a little crazy, and she thought she ought to straighten out her brain, just like Frankolin and Felicia ought to straighten out their house.

Where would the Sallys have gone? Why would they leave the house? Were they upset that they had been left behind? How would she ever find them? This was a big conundrum, probably the biggest conundrum in Baby's life so far. She needed a plan. She'd walk for a while longer until a plan came to her. Baby did her best thinking when she walked. If she had been allowed to walk in school, she'd probably have been an A+ student, but she mostly had to sit in school, so she was more of a B+ student.

On her ninety-sixth step she realized what she had to do. She needed to go back to her country house and sit where the Sallys had sat and think like a dog. That way she would know what they'd done. She would curl up in a tiny ball and think like a small dog, and get down on her hands and knees to think like a big dog. The time had come to stop walking and put out her thumb.

She looked at her thumb. She stuck it out, for practice, and then folded it back into her fist. Baby had never hitchhiked before. She'd heard her parents talking about the adventures they'd had hitchhiking around the country a long time ago. A long time ago no one had had rules against hitchhiking. Baby thought that hitchhiking might be illegal now, but she didn't care. She'd break the law to find her dogs. She'd do anything. She needed to get to the Sallys, and she needed a ride. If hitchhiking was the only way to get back to the country, she'd do it.

She watched as a large truck barreled down the road. She didn't want a ride in a big truck. It probably smelled like feet. She'd wait until a car that looked like it smelled better came along. After the big truck passed, she saw a green car. Baby didn't like the color green, so she didn't put out her thumb for the green car. Then a black car came. Who would ever buy a black car? And why didn't they make cars in prettier colors, anyway? How come you never saw pink cars or orange cars? Baby liked red cars the best. She decided that since the country was so far away, she should wait to hitchhike until a pink or orange or red car came by. That way she'd at least be riding in a good-color car. It would stink to be in a black car all the way to the country. Then she saw a red car, but her thumb got stuck and the car passed. The blue car behind it pulled over to the side of the road. Okay, the blue car wasn't just any blue car. It had a stripe. Okay, it also had a siren, and a man in a uniform driving.

"Excuse me," said the policeman. "Are you lost?"

"No, Officer," replied Baby. "I know exactly where I am."

Baby's heart pounded so loudly that she wanted to cover her ears. She didn't want to go to jail for hitchhiking; then she'd never see the Sallys again, or her mom, or her dad, or Tom. Life without Tom wouldn't be so bad. Life without Sally Squared would be terrible.

"Do you need a ride somewhere?"

"Yes!" she cried. "Are you going to arrest me?"

"Okay. Perhaps I can give you a ride. Where are you heading?" asked the policeman.

"I'm going to my country house in West Tipsbury. Are you going to arrest me?"

"West Tipsbury is a long way from here," commented the policeman.

"Yes, I know. I'm hoping to get a ride in an orange or pink or red car to make the trip more pleasant. Are you going to arrest me?"

"What do you think of blue cars?" asked the policeman.

"They're okay, I guess. Blue's nice. Are you going to arrest me?"

"That's good. I'm glad you like blue. So, are your parents at your country house?" asked the police officer.

"No. They're with some people at a pink and purple house. Are you going to arrest me?" Two red cars drove by. If the policeman wasn't planning on arresting her, she'd like to get back to her hitchhiking. She didn't want to miss all the red cars.

"Does that house belong to Frankolin and Felicia Allen?" asked the policeman.

"I think so," replied Baby.

"I think I'd better bring you back to your parents. It isn't safe for a young girl to be standing by the side of the road looking for a ride all by herself, and anyway, there aren't a lot of pink or orange or red cars around here."

Baby slumped her shoulders forward and followed the policeman to his car. It never happened like this on TV. On TV she would have had an adventure and found her dogs, and then met the policeman. He would have brought her and the dogs home to a hero's welcome. Baby knew what her mother would say about this story. "This isn't a Hollywood ending."

26
PAW PROBLEM

The Sallys strutted on.

They ambled down the road. Big Sally actually did the ambling, since little Sally was merely a passenger. A few cars passed, but amazingly, none stopped. You might think that the sight of a little dog riding on top of a big dog would stop hundreds of cars, but this strange sight clearly wasn't strange enough to stop any of the cars that drove by the two dogs on their way to the city. Perhaps the people in these cars had seen even stranger sights by the side of the road, like big dogs riding on the backs of little dogs. Or perhaps huge golden yellow *Ms* are the only things by the side of the road that get people to stop.

Little Sally quickly grew used to riding on big Sally's back. She tried out nine different riding positions. She rode sidesaddle and backward and with one paw in the air. If she walked carefully, she

could even pace the length of big Sally's entire long back.

As for big Sally, she started to think like a horse. At least she thought she was thinking like a horse. Before thinking like a horse, though, she had to figure out what a horse thought like. She wanted to think like a big horse, even though she was the same size as some small horses. First she imagined herself galloping through an emerald green field of grass. When she got tired, she rolled in a patch of bright yellow, orange, pink, and red wildflowers. Then she pictured herself competing in a race against the fastest horses in the world. Their hooves hit the ground and the earth trembled. Big Sally split from the pack. Her rider yelled out: "Go, girl. You're a champion." She crossed the finish line. Where were the other horses? Were they close by? No, not at all. The crowd cheered, "Sally! Sally! Sally!"

More hours and miles passed, just like the passing

of hours and miles when you're walking. That is to say, at first they passed quickly. Then time slowed down and they passed pretty slowly. After a while both dogs got used to the novelty of their situation. Little Sally stopped trying to find new positions, and big Sally stopped thinking like a horse. After a while the two dogs grew kind of bored.

"I don't want to complain, but my back left paw hurts," said big Sally.

"I know," replied little Sally.

"Really? Sometimes I feel like you know everything about me. Sometimes I feel like I don't even have to tell you things about me; you just know them. That's why you're my best friend," said big Sally. "Did you just know my paw was hurting? Was it like you could feel it hurting too?"

"Not really," said little Sally. "I've been watching blood come out of it, so I figured it must hurt."

"My paw is bleeding?" exclaimed big Sally.

"It's been bleeding for a while—for sixty-one steps, actually. I'm surprised it just started to hurt now. Do you think it takes big dogs longer to feel pain than small dogs? That would be unfair. You get to go that much longer before you feel a cut or a scrape or a bump, and life is better for that much longer than it is for a small dog who has the same cut or scrape or bump. If we banged our paws at the same time, you'd get to play for longer than me without even knowing you had hurt yourself. I'd be yelping and you'd still be chasing a ball. Big dogs have all the luck."

"Excuse me, but if I have all the luck, how come I'm walking around with a bleeding paw and you're having fun bouncing around on my back, without a bleeding paw? Who here is the lucky one?"

"I guess you have a point," said little Sally.

Big Sally howled. A sudden shooting pain whipped through her body. Blood dribbled out of her paw and trickled down the road, as if on its own journey, far away from big Sally's paw. Big Sally looked at the blood and wondered why it would want to travel so far from home. Big Sally certainly wouldn't have left home if the Puddles hadn't left without her. She would have rather been curled up by Baby's feet in the car, even if she did get cramps. She couldn't contain her grief any longer. She needed to rest. Her paw hurt. Blood spilled out of it, and little Sally let her bleed. How long would little Sally have let her keep walking while she was bleeding? What if she got an infection? Why had little Sally done this to her? Big Sally's brain felt sad and mad and confused. She had to figure out the answers to her questions, but her paw hurt and she needed a break from everything. She stopped walking and sat down. Little Sally lost her grip and tumbled off her back.

"Ouchy!"

"Oops. I forgot you were up there," said big Sally. "By the way, I guess you're right. It doesn't take you long to feel pain."

27

LITTLE SALLY

Her back hurt.

Her right front paw throbbed.

Her nose stung.

Her hurts hurt.

Little Sally glared at big Sally. How could that overgrown excuse for a dog have let her fall? What kind of friend would do that to another friend, even if they had had a tiny disagreement? Not a real friend. Little Sally furiously began to calculate her options.

Option #1:
She could leave big Sally. She gave that an 8. And walk back to the house in the country alone. She gave that a 1.
Option #2:
She could leave big Sally (8) and walk to the city alone (1).

Option #3:
She could stay with big Sally (1) and they could go to the city together without being best friends (8). They could be more like business partners.

Option #1:
$8 + 1 = 9$
Option #2:
$8 + 1 = 9$
Option #3:
$1 + 8 = 9$

She did the math, but all her options added up to the same thing. How could she decide which option to take if they all added up to nine? Fine. She'd decide another way. Maybe she'd flip a coin. Of course she didn't have a coin to flip or a thumb with which to flip it. Forget it; she didn't need a coin. She didn't need anything. She really didn't need big Sally, who'd made her fall. She couldn't even remember why she'd ever wanted to be friends with such a big, clumsy, mean dog. She'd only become friends with big Sally because there hadn't been any other dogs around. Well, that wasn't totally true. They did have dogs in the neighborhood, but Napoléon was a pit bull, and who wanted to be friends with a pit bull? He'd act all nice and friendly, like he wanted to play, but if you ever said something he didn't like, he'd flash his teeth at you so you'd remember exactly what you were dealing with. Being friends with big Sally was a lot better than being friends with Napoléon, that was for sure. And Huck was annoying. Little Sally had never figured out how a Chihuahua mix could be so annoying. Huck was only interested in letting everyone know that he was bigger than little Sally, as if dogs couldn't see that for themselves. It was pretty obvious, but no, Huck still needed to bring it up every time they were together. He gave Chihuahuas a bad name. He must have been mixed with some really annoying breed of dog, probably a Great Dane. Maybe big Sally wasn't as bad as some other dogs, but a real best friend wouldn't have suddenly sat down without warning and let little Sally tumble off her back.

The Sallys sat back to back, ignoring each other, until big Sally broke the silence.

"What are you doing?"

"Thinking," said little Sally.

"What are you thinking?"

"I'm thinking that if I wanted to tell you what I was thinking, I'd be doing my thinking out loud, but since I'm doing my thinking to myself, I probably don't want to share my thoughts," snapped little Sally.

Big Sally sat quietly for a few moments trying to figure out exactly what little Sally had meant by her last remark. "So that's what you were thinking?"

"No."

"Then, why'd you say that when I asked 'What are you thinking?'"

Little Sally stood up. She'd had enough of big Sally. She wanted to be alone. She couldn't even stand being on the same side of the road as big Sally. It made her feel itchy. She needed to get away and decided to cross the street. She picked up her little paws and made a dash for it. Midway across, they heard a horrible screeching sound.

28

WHAT HAPPENED NEXT

Big Sally yelped. The pickup truck skidded to a stop. Big Sally felt glued to the ground but managed to pull her legs free. The driver jumped out of his pickup truck. A tiny something or other lay shaking in the middle of the road. The driver dropped down to the ground and put his head against the pavement to get a better look at what seemed to be a fruit-fly-size dog. Big Sally poked at little Sally with her nose. Little Sally trembled. The driver stared at the quivering dog, his face mere inches from her.

Little Sally opened her eyes to find out if she was still alive. She saw big Sally's long nose and soupy black eyes and a strange man's freckly nose and sky blue eyes inches away from her face. She couldn't remember what had happened or how long she'd been trembling in the middle of the road, but she suddenly felt a little embarrassed, so she got up and finished crossing the street.

Big Sally barked, and the man in the pickup truck smiled and said, "Hey, pups. Are you lost? Are you hungry? Come on. Jump in."

29

THE RETURN OF BABY

The doorbell rang. Felicia swung open the front door and saw Baby's frowning face next to a shiny badge.

"Oh, did you get lost coming back from the bathroom?" she asked.

Baby didn't say anything. The policeman introduced himself.

"Mrs. Allen, sorry to bother you. I'm Officer Randall. This young woman said her parents are visiting you. Are they available?"

Felicia excused herself and returned with Mr. and Mrs. Puddle.

"Emily?" said Mrs. Puddle.

"Ferdinanda?" said Mr. Puddle.

"Is this your daughter?" asked the policeman.

Mrs. Puddle jumped forward and threw her arms around Baby.

118

Mr. Puddle filled the policeman in on the details of the day's events, hoping he'd understand their predicament and offer to drive them back to the country. As Mr. Puddle talked, he did the calculations in his head.

If a regular car going fifty miles per hour takes almost an hour and twenty minutes to go seventy miles, how long would it take a police car with the sirens blaring going one hundred miles per hour?

A: Less than an hour
B: More than an hour
C: An hour

When he figured out the answer, his lips shifted toward the sky.

The policeman listened to Mr. Puddle's story carefully. He did a lot of nodding and aha-ing. Then he said, "Good luck. Keep track of your children, and try to keep better track of your dogs. I'll be going now."

The door slammed behind him.

30

THE MAP

"First let me present the map," said Frankolin. He held up a roll of brightly colored paper. "Okay, clear the decks. Sweep the rugs under the dust so we may study our options."

Frankolin's wife, Felicia, darted around the room tossing dust balls on top of the rug and sweeping trinkets and clothes and books and all sorts of other stuff under the rug. She picked up a boot, a lamp shade, a baseball glove, a bicycle wheel, a broom, and a saddle.

You name it, she picked it up.

You name it:

_____.

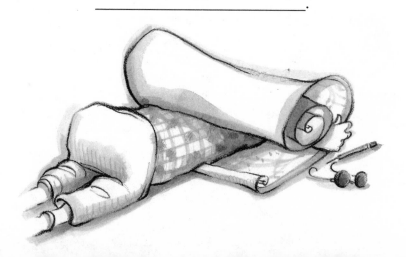

When a clearing on the rug appeared, Frankolin unrolled the map. "We are here. Show me where you live."

"This is my house," said Baby, who spotted her house immediately on the map.

"Aha, ahem, hatchoo. So your dogs, they must be between, betwixt, or beyond, near here or away from there. What we know is they've left their home. They've vacated, evacuated, and immaculated. What we don't know is if they left on their own or if they were snatched by evil dog snatchers wearing rumpled clothes. If they left by themselves, did they turn left or right? Did they walk or run? Are they together or alone? On the island or off? Are they—no, I cannot say. But I must say. We must look at the possibilities, the fractions, and the math facts. Then we'll deduct the probabilities from the possibilities. What if the news is bad? Could they be? No! I cannot say. I must say. Okay, I'll say. But the young girl must cover her ears. She is too young, too innocent, too, too, too . . . Two times two is four and four score and seven years ago was the happiest year of my life, even if I wasn't born yet. Ah, I digress, I regress. I am dressed. I'm sorry. Little girl, please cover your ears."

Baby loosely cupped her hands over her ears. She could still hear everything Frankolin was saying, but she wanted him to think she couldn't. She glanced at the floor because she thought someone who really couldn't hear would either look down at the floor or up at the ceiling. She noticed a caterpillar trying to forge its way over one of the dust balls.

Frankolin looked at Baby. A tear formed in the corner of his left eye and dripped down his cheek. He didn't believe children needed to hear about life's challenges. Why should a child have to learn about war or death or all the other difficult issues that adults worry so much about? It would just confuse them, and confusion is so confusing. He took a deep breath, double-checked to make sure Baby couldn't hear, and then whispered, "Are they still alive?"

31
MAN IN A TRUCK

"Get in," commanded the man who had almost run over little Sally.

Little Sally looked down at the ground. She tapped her paw on the pavement. She breathed in the exhaust fumes from the pickup truck. She sneezed.

"Come on. I don't have all day. Hop on in."

Neither dog budged.

"I've got treats," said the man.

Big Sally jumped into the truck.

Little Sally couldn't believe her eyes. It was as if big Sally would have done anything for a treat, even get into a strange man's truck. Little Sally marveled at the ridiculous things she'd seen big Sally do for one measly treat. She simply couldn't understand how a dog could be foolish enough to come, sit, stay, jump, come again, sit, lie down, give a paw, roll over, lie down, stay, come, give a paw, roll over, turn around, turn around again, give a paw, just for food.

Who needed it? Little Sally had far more dignity. Sure, she'd occasionally come for a treat, but she'd never act like a circus clown. She refused to sit or lie down and do all that other twirling and rolling and flipping and flopping stuff. Ugh. How embarrassing. If she really wanted a treat, all she had to do was look up at the treat giver with her big brown eyes and tilt her head slightly to the side. No one could resist the head tilt. People liked to say, "Little dogs don't do tricks." But the truth is little dogs have more self-respect than big dogs. Little Sally would have never lowered herself to jump into a pickup truck simply for a treat. No, not little Sally. To show her defiance, she sat with her back toward the pickup truck while big Sally gnawed away on a delicious kibble in the front seat.

"What's wrong with your friend?" asked the man. "Is she playing hard to get?" He handed big Sally another dog treat.

Fine, thought little Sally. *I'll get into the truck, but only so big Sally doesn't look like such a pig. I don't want her to feel bad that she's eating all the treats and hasn't shared one with me. I'm sure she'd feel awful about that, especially after all the other terrible things she's done to me today. I better get in for big Sally's sake.*

Little Sally looked up and up and up. The distance between the tip of her nose and the floor of the truck seemed to be about the same as the distance between the tip of her nose and the moon. Oh, well, she'd give it a shot. She put all her weight on her hind legs, took a deep breath, and sprang up as high as her paws would take her, but she didn't come close to reaching the truck. Her springer couldn't spring her high enough. She jumped again and again and again.

"It looks to me like your friend had a change of heart." The man reached down and plucked little Sally off the ground. "You can sit right on my lap."

Little Sally closed one eye, twitched her nose, and growled. She figured it was in her best interest to make sure the man realized from the start that, unlike big Sally, she had high standards. Little Sally knew better than to be nice to just anyone. If you were nice to anyone, before you knew it, you'd have to be nice to everyone, and a little dog can't afford to be nice to everyone. Imagine how many times you'd be dropped if you let everyone play with you or, worse yet, how many times you'd be tossed into the air because you're as small as a ball. Little dogs need to be careful.

This man didn't even know how to drive his truck without almost running someone over. He still had a lot of work to do before he proved he was worthy as a lap pillow. In fact, little Sally decided she wouldn't even wag her tail for him.

32

ON THE ROAD AGAIN

The two dogs bounced along in the passenger seat. Big Sally figured that now that they had a ride, they'd be in the city before she could finish her treats. She chewed and chewed, and after a few minutes of vigorous gnawing, she stopped thinking about getting to the city.

The man driving the truck leaned over. Big Sally sat still as he reached across her back and fumbled with her collar. Little Sally growled and snapped her teeth together when his hand strayed close to her collar. She'd allow him the pleasure of giving her treats, but that's all. No tail wagging, no lap sitting, and no looking at tags on her collar.

They pulled off the main road and onto a bumpy dirt driveway. Big Sally pricked up her ears. Where was he taking them? This wasn't the road to the city? Or was it? Maybe this was a shortcut. The dogs flopped around the inside of the truck as it dipped in holes and rebounded out. Big Sally's head almost hit the windshield. Little Sally glared at the bad driver. She shot him her you-must-be-the-worst-driver-ever look. He must have noticed, because he stopped the truck.

Big Sally glanced out the window and saw a large garden attached to a small house. Little Sally noticed that big Sally's paw had stopped bleeding. Big Sally barked.

"Shhh. Quiet." The man looked over at the dogs. "I'm getting out for a few minutes," he said. But he didn't move. He didn't get out of the truck. He didn't start looking for his wallet or check to see what he looked like in the mirror. He sat still and watched the Sallys as they gobbled down more treats.

"All right," he said. "I guess I'd better get this done if I'm still a secret catcher." He dropped a handful of bacon bits onto the seat of the truck, opened the door, and walked toward the house.

Big Sally watched him as she chewed. Little Sally couldn't see out the window, so big Sally reported what was going on.

"He's walking.

"He's standing in front of the door.

"He's looking back at us.

"He turned around.

"I think he's knocking on the door.

"Nothing's happening.

"Now someone's opening a door.

"It's a lady.

"I don't see a dog.

"They're talking.

"Hey, what's a secret catcher, anyway?"

Little Sally looked up at big Sally and rolled her eyes. "I can't believe you don't know what a secret catcher is. It's just like a dogcatcher, only they catch secrets instead of dogs."

"Really?"

"Yes. Really."

"So are we catching a secret now?"

"Of course," said little Sally.

"Oh," said big Sally. "He's coming back. I don't see anything. I don't know what the secret looks like."

"They tend to be blue. Do you see anything blue? I bet this one is ugly," said little Sally. "I hope it's small. Small secrets are the best to catch."

"Really? Why?" asked big Sally.

"Because they're small," answered little Sally.

"I like big secrets," big Sally said with a sigh. "Did you see that?"

"Of course I didn't see that. What happened?"

"The lady ran after him and bopped him."

"She bopped him?"

"Big bop. Here he comes. He's running. She's running after him. Duck!"

"I don't need to duck. I'm already down here."

The door to the truck flung open and the man threw himself in. He spun the truck around and sped away.

The man coughed out a few words as they bumped and bounced their way back to the main road.

"Had to tell."

Bump.

"Secrets destroy."

Bump.

Bump.

Bump.

"Had to do it."

33

THE SECRET CATCHER

Scott, the man driving the pickup truck that had almost run over little Sally, didn't go secret catching every day, and he certainly didn't almost run over a tiny Chihuahua every day. Most days he worked in his bookstore. He shelved books. He read. And he talked to customers. That's where he usually found out about the secrets lurking in town. By being around books, a secret catcher can keep tabs on the great secrets in literature and keep up-to-date on the local scene as well. If he'd had his way, Oaks Bluff would have been a secret-free town. People from all over the world would go there when they wanted to escape from secrets. People who lived there would abide by a strict no-hiding-anything law. They'd pledge to tell all their old secrets and keep no new secrets. He didn't care if their secrets were good or bad; he wanted them out of his town. But until that happened, he'd do his part to limit the number of secrets wandering through the narrow streets and passing through the front doors of stores and sneaking into attics and other places secrets tended to linger.

A lot of people in town hung out in his bookstore. They'd buy books and blab their secrets. Most people like to see secrets revealed but don't want to do the revealing themselves. They'd prefer to tell the secrets to someone who doesn't believe secrets should ever be kept. Telling secrets to an official secret catcher made people feel like they were off the hook. He could spill their secrets for them.

Of course, not everyone liked secret catchers. Some people plan for their secrets to remain secret. That's what they are, after all—secrets. These people say a secret catcher has no right to come into their lives and expose their private, personal, and most secret of secrets. Once, someone got so angry that she tried to have Scott the secret catcher arrested for stealing a secret.

34

THE STORY OF WHEN THE SECRET CATCHER ALMOST GOT ARRESTED

Anna Marino had red hair and green eyes and always wore black clothes. She moved to the small town of Oaks Bluff when she was twelve. By the time she turned thirty, she'd been divorced four times. It's true that all four of her husbands left her, but Anna Marino wasn't a bad person, she just had issues. She liked to lie and she enjoyed keeping secrets. Neither of these traits were particularly helpful in a marriage. All four of her ex-husbands preferred honesty. One of them once told her, "I think you'll lie about anything, even the weather." Another husband once said, "Can you tell me what we're having for dinner, or is that a secret too?"

Sometimes Anna Marino did nice things for people and kept it a secret. She once bought a bike for a child in town whose parents were out of work, and she anonymously left it on their front porch. And she once went to the park in the middle of the night and picked up all the litter. But more often than not, Anna Marino's secrets and lies hurt people.

Scott tried to expose her secrets before they did too much harm, but with so many secrets, there wasn't enough time in the day. The week before Anna Marino was scheduled to marry her fifth husband, Scott found out that Anna Marino was keeping a giant secret. A secret so big that it loomed larger and longer and was more mystifying than the blank part of this page. . . .

And this blank page.

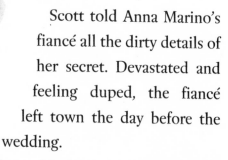

Scott told Anna Marino's fiancé all the dirty details of her secret. Devastated and feeling duped, the fiancé left town the day before the wedding.

Anna Marino got so upset she called the police and demanded they arrest Scott for stealing a valuable secret.

The police officer that answered her call had a hard time understanding the nature of the crime.

"How big was the secret? When did it disappear?" asked the police officer. "What did the secret look like? Where did you get it? Where was it located when it was stolen? What is its value? Was the house locked? And what was the secret, anyway?"

Anna Marino refused to tell the policeman her secret. So the policeman said, "There isn't enough evidence to make an arrest."

A fuming Anna Marino decided to take matters into her own hands. She woke up at three o'clock in the morning and slipped out of her house into town. The last person in town had strolled through an hour and a half earlier. The only cars around were parked cars. The only lights on were night-lights. Anna Marino had the town to herself. When she got to Scott's bookstore, she kicked the door. Then she pulled a can of neon orange spray paint out of her bag and scrawled these words across the entire front of the store:

Before she finished painting the "iness" in "business," a young mother by the name of Lucinda Maple drove by and spotted her.

Why was Lucinda Maple driving around in the middle of the night? Well, anyone who knew Lucinda Maple would tell you that Lucinda Maple's baby would fall asleep only in the car. So Lucinda and her husband spent much of their day and many of their nights on snooze cruises. Lucinda's baby had just dozed off when Lucinda drove down Main Street past the bookstore at three sixteen in the morning.

She stopped the car and whispered in her loudest whisper, "Hey, who's that? What are you doing?"

Anna Marino whispered back, "Shhhh. Don't tell anyone. It's a secret."

Silly Anna Marino. Did she really think she could keep a secret from a secret catcher? The next day a policeman knocked on Anna Marino's front door. He handcuffed her and brought her to the police station.

Anna Marino spent ten nights in jail.

There is more to say about Anna, but we'll save that for another day or maybe even another book.

35

ANOTHER TALE

Scott turned left. He handed bones to both dogs. The pickup truck started to climb up a windy mountain road but then zipped down a long hill before any ears had a chance to clog up. The truck passed a baseball field without players, and a cow farm. Out of habit Scott slowed down as he approached the post office. He nodded his head and smiled. It was at this post office that he had caught one of the most important secrets in his career as a secret catcher.

In the fall, about a week after the Detroit Tigers won the World Series, nine-year-old Molly Flam received a nasty letter. Over the course of the next three weeks, she got three more letters. All of them bore the same signature, from A-non-eye-mouse. Each letter said something mean about Molly. One told her that she smelled like stinky fish water. Another letter claimed she did terrible cartwheels and didn't know how to walk too well either. The third letter said her dog was ugly. The fourth letter predicted that no one would ever want to be friends with her again. All the letters had a picture on them of a mouse with no eye.

As one could imagine, these letters upset Molly terribly. She hated mail time. She stopped wanting to go to school. And she started taking three showers a day to ensure that she didn't smell like stinky fish water.

Molly's mother, an avid reader and book buyer, told the secret catcher about the letters from A-non-eye-mouse. He vowed to help. He believed that the longer a secret festered, the bigger it grew, and the biggest secrets eventually exploded. He knew this from firsthand experience. He thought this secret could be on the verge of exploding. And he worried that poor Molly would surely turn into a prune if she took any more showers. To catch this secret, he needed to spend his days watching the comings and goings at the post office.

People arrived holding envelopes. They left carrying packages. Most people had a post office routine. They'd show up at the same time day after day. Molly's mother and Molly's aunt Samantha and cousin Sam walked in at 3:15 p.m. each day. That was their routine. Day after day, until Thursday.

Thursday at 4:45 p.m., little Sam walked into the post office alone holding a small blue envelope. At 4:48 he walked out.

Friday at 3:15, Molly, her mother, Aunt Samantha, and Cousin Sam arrived as usual.

Molly's mother flipped through the mail. She saw bills, a magazine, and a small blue envelope addressed to Molly.

"You should open it," said her mother.

Molly squinted. Her nose looked red. She separated the envelope from the note as carefully as her grandmother unwrapped presents on Christmas. Then she read the note and ripped it to shreds.

Sam chuckled.

"Sam," scolded his mother. "It's not funny."

"Sorry." Sam shrugged. The boy looked down at the ground so his mother couldn't see the giant smile running rampant across his face.

Molly bolted across the parking lot.

Her mother dashed after her.

Scott scooted over to Sam and his mother.

"Sam, why don't you help me put this note back together?" he asked.

"Don't want to," said Sam. "Come on, Ma. We gotta go." He tugged on her sleeve.

Sam's mother looked astonished, as if she'd never heard Sam act rude before. Of course, she had, but she preferred that people think Sam was a perfect child. That was her little secret, because Sam was not only not a perfect child, he could be a perfectly terrible child.

"Sam, please help pick up the pieces of paper. I don't care how upset your cousin Molly is; she shouldn't litter."

"I wouldn't litter," said Sam.

"I know you wouldn't litter," repeated Sam's mother, just to make sure the secret catcher heard what her son had said.

The three of them collected the scraps of paper and pieced them together.

Dear Molly,
You look like a mouse.
From,
A-non-eye-mouse

"Sam, doesn't that look like our mouse, Moo-Moo?" asked his mother.

"Naw," said Sam. "Come on, Ma. I wanna go now."

"Wait one second," said his mother. She pushed her face closer to the scraps of paper and examined the mouse. "That's our Moo-Moo. Someone took a picture of Moo-Moo and is using him on these terrible letters. Sam, look what one of your friends has done."

"Uh, yeah, Mom. Doesn't really look like Moo-Moo to me."

"Of course that's Moo-Moo, Sam."

Scott turned to Sam. "Did you come here yesterday and mail a letter to Molly? I saw you at the post office all by yourself."

"No way. No way! I wouldn't do that. No way. Anyway, if I did, which I didn't, she deserves it. She does smell like stinky fish water. Ma, let's get out of here. Come on, Ma."

Sam pulled on his mother's hand, and this time she trailed off behind him, calling out, "Oh, my, look at the time. We must be off. Sam has to practice his cello. He's very talented, probably a prodigy."

Of course Scott didn't know for sure, but on a scale from one to ten, he gave it a ten that Molly Flam wouldn't be getting any more letters from A-non-eye-mouse.

THE SILENT RIDE

The mechanic called Mrs. Puddle back. The car needed a new part. An old part had sputtered out. "You bet," said the mechanic. "It's lucky I caught it. The replacement part will arrive in a day or two. Not to worry, ma'am. She'll be as good as new, maybe better. I'll even clean her for you. That's on me."

"That solves it," said Frankolin. "I'll take you myself. I promised. I vowed. I told you and you and you and you that I'd help find your dogs, and that's what I'll do."

Within minutes the four Puddles, Frankolin, and the king were fighting over who was going to sit where in Frankolin's tiny car. Mr. Puddle and Mrs. Puddle couldn't agree on who should sit in the front seat. Baby's and Tom's knees banged against their noses in the backseat, and their fists kept landing on each other's arms. Mr. Puddle tried sitting between them, but he got a cramp in his leg and yelled.

Mrs. Puddle thought he was being overly dramatic and told him he'd be fine. Mr. Puddle argued that he'd end up in the hospital if he had to sit in the backseat. Mrs. Puddle wedged herself in between Baby and Tom. Mr. Puddle said, "See, your legs are shorter than mine."

Mrs. Puddle said, "But I get carsick. I shouldn't sit in the back."

So Mr. Puddle squeezed into the backseat again and started complaining about his back. "I'm not sitting in the backseat."

"Neither am I," said Mrs. Puddle.

Baby pleaded, "Please, Mom, just try. We'll never get going unless someone sits between me and Tom."

"Fine, Emily, but just for a short while." She settled in between Baby and Tom and sighed a long loud sigh so that everyone in the car knew the extent of her misery. Mr. Puddle felt pleased his wife had decided to sit in the backseat, and started to hum. He got in the front seat and stretched his back. The king sat on his lap. Frankolin drove.

"Here's the plan," shouted Frankolin. His loud

voice ricocheted around the small car and then escaped out one of the windows.

"By the end of 1:13 p.m., we will be heading south. If anyone hears a dog, sees a dog, or smells a dog, let the driver know. That's me. If anyone is a dog, let the driver know. That's me."

"Woof," barked the king.

"Thank you. Here sits the king. When he barks once, we'll turn left. If he gives us two barks, we'll know to turn right. More than two barks means we stop. We let him out. He smells the ground. He smells the air. When he lifts a leg, it's a sign and we'll know which direction to follow."

Frankolin jammed the car into gear and off they went. The king held his head high and peered out of the window. Silently.

Silently some more.

Still silently after ten miles.

Silent for another forty miles.

The king didn't bark or growl or talk or meow or do anything at all. He sat silently. The silence went on for such a long time and got so silent that it started to sound loud . . .

and louder . . .

and louder . . .

until the king broke the loud silence. After a total of seventy-two miles, the king barked twice.

THE KING'S BARK

"Finally," said Baby. "He barked. Let's turn."

Mrs. Puddle groaned. "I can't believe we're listening to a d-o-g. I cannot believe it. Cannot. Cannot. C-a-n-n-o-t. Will not. Cannot. Is this really happening? We left our dogs on an island. They are surely still on that island. We are not turning down this road."

Frankolin's face grew long. His jowls sunk down. His shoulders smacked up against his ears. His eyes drooped like a Saint Bernard's. While his face stretched out, his already small body seemed to shrivel up. His legs quivered nervously like a greyhound's. "She's right. It's a bad place to turn. After all, what does the king know? Nothing. That's what he knows. Nothing. He's only human, except that he's a dog. And how is it to be human, even if you are a dog? Humans make mistakes. No dog would be human without mistakes, even if they are a dog. And I'll tell you why we shouldn't turn: Because he made a mistake, and everyone knows that a mistake a day keeps the doctor away."

"Apple," piped in Baby.

"Ah, of course. A mistake a day keeps the apples away."

"An apple keeps the doctor away," said Baby.

"Ah, and the doctor will give one stitch not nine."

"No, the doctor stays away with an apple a day. A stitch in time saves nine."

"Nine stitches. What a large cut. I hope it didn't hurt too much."

"I didn't cut myself," huffed Baby. "I think we should turn."

"The king made a mistake. Even kings make mistakes. When Louis XVI was king, he made lots of mistakes. His mistakes were so terrible, they cost him his head. We don't want our king to lose his head. One headless dogman is more than enough."

"It's a headless horseman, and you said we'd turn when he barked twice," insisted Baby.

"I also said he's made a mistake, an error, a

blunder, a slipup. He's wrong, incorrect, mistaken, and erroneous, and all the other cinnamons in the thesaurus."

"Don't you mean synonyms?" asked Baby quietly.

"Yes, synonyms. Like I said, the king is only human."

"Except he's a dog," chimed in Baby.

"But," said Mrs. Puddle, a tad mischievously, "you did say we must listen to the king."

"If Frankolin thinks the dog has made a mistake, let's keep driving," said Mr. Puddle.

"I've changed my mind. Let's turn here," insisted Mrs. Puddle. Baby thought her mother was trying to disagree just because they'd gone almost an hour without a disagreement. "Let's listen to the king. That's why we've crammed five people and a dog into a ridiculously—I mean delightfully—tiny car. This is why we're doing this, to listen to the king, right? Question mark."

"Mom," growled Baby. Sometimes Mrs. Puddle drove Baby crazy. Why couldn't she just be quiet? Why did she need to argue all the time? Why couldn't she just say, "Okay, fine with me," for once?

"I said, let's turn right," repeated Mrs. Puddle. Her voice sounded as though she had just drank a cup of lemon juice. This lemony juice voice could move mountains, or at least move Baby to clean her room and brush her teeth. Amazingly, it didn't seem to have the same effect on Frankolin.

"No!" snapped Frankolin. "We can't turn down that road."

38

COMPROMISE ROAD

The Puddles strained their necks to peer down the road Frankolin refused to take. The sign on the corner said COMPROMISE ROAD.

Compromise Road was neither straight nor curvy. It was neither long nor short. Brightly colored wildflowers and tall trees, mostly oaks, lined the left side of the road. Evergreens, generally white pines, lined the right side of the road. As they passed by, the four Puddles all processed the same thought. Each one of them wanted to drive down Compromise Road. On a scale of one to ten, they all wanted it a ten.

No one said anything, but if desire could have turned a car around, Frankolin's car would have swung a U-ey. Desire can't turn a car around, though, and Frankolin's car didn't turn. It kept going straight.

Why is it that the things you aren't supposed to know about always seem so much more interesting

than the things you are
allowed to know about?

Write your answer here:

_____

How is it that the words "we can't go down
that road" can make four people determined to go
down the road that they were just told they can't
go down? If Frankolin had said, "That road is a dead
end," or if he had said, "There are falling boulders
on that road and it's not safe so we shouldn't go
down it," that would have squelched the Puddles'
desire to go down Compromise Road. But he didn't
say either of those things. He said, "We can't turn
down that road." And all four Puddles wanted to
know why. What was down Compromise Road?

Baby thought that a big scary monster must live down the road.

Tom thought Frankolin must have a treasure chest filled with gold coins hidden at the end of the road and he didn't want them to find out about it.

Mrs. Puddle thought that Frankolin's ex-wife lived down the road.

Mr. Puddle didn't know what to think. He could only think about how much he wanted to go down that road.

Baby started thinking more about the big monster. What if he had blue curly hair and six eyes and ate children? What if he ate dogs? What if the Sallys were roasting in his big monster oven and he planned on eating them for dinner? Baby got so scared thinking about the disgusting mean dog-eating monster that she forgot to breathe.

"Look, Baby's turning blue," commented Tom. "She looks pretty."

"What?" asked Mrs. Puddle. She looked over at her daughter and saw that Baby's face had turned a slight bluish purplish shade. "Breathe, Emily. Breathe."

Baby turned her head toward her mother. Her

mother's face looked mushy, like a bowl of mashed potatoes.

"Breathe, Emily," said the bowl of mashed potatoes in a loving tone.

Baby opened her mouth. Oxygen rushed in.

AGREEMENT

"Can we please pull over?" asked Mrs. Puddle.

Frankolin looked nervous. Six beads of sweat grasped onto his forehead and filled up like balloons on the verge of popping. Without saying a word, he pulled off the main road. The car jolted to a stop.

"Let's take a little walk, Emily," said Mrs. Puddle.

"Tom, you and I should also get out and stretch our legs," said Mr. Puddle.

"That's a wonderful idea, honey," said Mrs. Puddle.

"Thanks," said Mr. Puddle.

Baby and Tom looked at each other. Could it be? Yes, it certainly sounded like their parents had just agreed on something. For a moment, Baby was so surprised she forgot to breathe again.

"Ferdinanda, please take a breath. Maybe we can all stretch our legs and take a little walk together," suggested Mr. Puddle.

"That's another wonderful idea," chirped Mrs. Puddle.

Mr. and Mrs. Puddle had just agreed twice, thereby eliminating two ten-minute arguments over who should get out of the car, who should walk, and who shouldn't. Two agreements in less than two minutes. One agreement per minute. That must have been a new record or something.

The Puddles got out of the car and strolled over to the edge of the woods, but before they got too far, an egg-shaped cloud formed above them and rumbled loudly. They looked up. The egg cracked in half and released a torrent of rain. Baby and Tom and Mr. and Mrs. Puddle scurried back to Frankolin's car as fast as they could.

DOWN COMPROMISE ROAD

The Puddles and Frankolin sat slouched shoulder to slouched shoulder in the Bug and waited for the rain to pass. Raindrops splattered across the windshield. Baby watched the shapes. She saw bunnies and dogs and frogs, and then she saw the big scary monster that probably had just put a dash of salt and pepper on the Sallys. Baby thought about how scared they must be. She couldn't imagine that they'd taste good, even to a monster.

Frankolin let out several deep long sighs before speaking.

"I don't know how to say this. I cannot, but I must. I shouldn't, yet I have to. I don't want to, but I will. I wish I didn't have to, but I want to. I can't. It's complicated.

"I will.
No, I won't.
Yes, I have to.

I'm going to say it.

Here I go.

Wait. I can't.

Let me try again.

Here I go.

Nope. Couldn't do it that time either.

One last try.

Here goes. I'm going to—

Ah, it doesn't work.

This is either my final or my last attempt.

Here I go.

My son lives down that road.

There. I did it."

None of the Puddles knew what to say.

They could have said something like, "Oh, really."

They could have said something like, "I'm sorry."

But why would they? All Frankolin had said was, "My son lives down that road." Except the tone he'd used had made them feel sorry.

Their other option was to say nothing at all, which is what they decided to say. Not to say that they said the words "nothing at all." They just remained silent. That is, until Mrs. Puddle changed her mind and decided to say, "How nice for you."

Everyone, even the king, knew that of all the things to say, "How nice for you" was not the right thing to say.

The king barked in disgust. Baby groaned. Tom moaned, Mr. Puddle sighed, and Frankolin began to sob.

"Not nice. No. Noooooooooooooooo. Ohhhhh, noooooo. It's not nice at all. My son, my son, my son despises me like a mouse despises a cat."

Now the time seemed right to say "I'm sorry." So they did. Except for Mrs. Puddle.

"Then I guess maybe you're right," said Mrs. Puddle. "We probably shouldn't turn right there, I mean with your son hating you so much. I can't imagine anything so terrible. It must be a-w-f-u-l, awful for you. Why does he hate you so? Did you do something terrible?" The king barked in disgust. Baby groaned again. Tom moaned again, Mr. Puddle sighed again, and Frankolin kept crying.

Mr. Puddle hoped to mollify Frankolin. "I'm

sure you were wonderful parents. Do you want a few minutes alone?"

Frankolin stepped out of the car and slammed the door shut. He got back into the car and slammed the door shut. Out of the car,  into the car, out, in, out, in, out until he closed the car door on his finger and yelled, "MARVIN ANTHILL DIAPER!"

Frankolin got back in and put both hands on the steering wheel. His pointer finger throbbed like a panting dog. His eyes fogged up. He carefully placed his right foot on the accelerator and pushed down. "The king is never wrong. My son collects dogs. He probably has yours."

41

FRANKOLIN'S SECRET

Baby couldn't believe it. Frankolin's son might have the Sallys. Maybe they hadn't gotten dog-napped by a monster. She imagined how happy they'd be to see her. Big Sally would jump up and drape her paws over Baby's shoulders, and little Sally would jump up with her paws on Baby's ankles.

Frankolin turned the car around and drove down Compromise Road. The Puddles sat perfectly still. Some people might have described the car as quiet enough to hear a pin drop. Frankolin thought the car was quiet enough to hear dew drop. Of course, dew doesn't tend to drop, but Frankolin's confusion had never stopped him before, and it wasn't going to stop him now. He closed one of his misty eyes and tried looking backward. He remembered the most golden day of his life. On that day he and Felicia brought their two-day-old son home from the hospital. The boy had a tuft of red hair and a twinkle in his left eye. Frankolin and Felicia both thought he smiled the first time he saw them. The nurse said it was gas. They named him Scott.

As a toddler Scott loved to climb on furniture and play with anything that rolled. He didn't talk much but smiled often. His parents didn't want to confuse him, so they decided not to tell him he was adopted until his fifth birthday. Then his fifth birthday came and went and they never mentioned it. So they decided to tell him on his seventh birthday, which also came and went without a mention. So they decided to wait a while longer before telling him. Ten seemed like an appropriate age, until ten came and it no longer seemed appropriate. By the time he'd turned thirteen, they'd decided they shouldn't tell him at all because he'd get too confused. Why should they burden their smiling boy? They decided to keep his adoption a secret. Frankolin knew what it felt like to feel confused, as he spent most of his life in a befuddled state. Scott was their son anyway. Did it really matter that he'd come from an adoption agency instead of from Felicia? They raised him. They helped him with his homework, taught him how to ride a bike, and took him on camping trips. They never forced him to make his bed or clean his room. They loved him, and they decided he never needed to know about his adoption.

Other people knew, though. It never dawned on Frankolin and Felicia that someone would spill their secret. But sure enough, spill they did.

On his eighteenth birthday Scott went out to dinner with his girlfriend, Debby. He had just cracked his lobster when Debby said, "Do you ever wonder about your real parents?"

"What are you talking about?" asked Scott.

Debby repeated her question, "Do you ever wonder about your real parents? Do you ever think about what they are like or who they are?"

"What are you talking about?" asked Scott again.

"If you don't want to talk about being adopted, we don't have to," said Debby.

"I wasn't adopted," responded Scott.

Debby started feeling queasy, but continued talking anyway. "You don't look like your parents because you're kind of, you know, adopted."

Scott replied snippily: "No, you know, I'm telling you. I kind of wasn't."

Debby's face contorted. "I figured you knew. It seems so obvious. Think about it. You like things clean and orderly. Your parents love messes. You have red hair and blue eyes and freckles. They don't. Look how tall you are and how short your father is."

"My mom's tall," said Scott.

"They should have told you," said Debby as she nervously grappled with a piece of lamb.

Scott didn't finish his dinner that night. Instead he broke up with Debby and went home.

When he walked through the door, Frankolin and Felicia surprised him with a joyous round of "Happy Birthday" and a six-layer chocolate cake. Scott blew out the candles and said, "My wish is to know the truth. Was I adopted?"

"That's your wish? Really?" Frankolin asked, and gulped.

"Really," said Scott.

Felicia nervously inserted a candle into a curl in her hair. "We didn't know how to tell you." Felicia took a deep breath, grabbed the candle, and continued on. "We adopted you. We thought you might get confused if we told you, so we kept it a secret. You know your father gets confused so easily, and he didn't want you to be confused too." She smiled lovingly at Scott. Her curly hair bounced up and down and her lips pushed her cheeks closer to her eyes.

Scott frowned. He hated secrets, and he hated his parents for keeping this secret from him.

That night he packed up his room. By morning he had moved out.

At first he let Frankolin and Felicia visit him. He wouldn't talk to them, but he allowed them to talk to him. Then he decided he didn't even want them to talk to him, so he bought a mean dog with yellow teeth and a baritone growl. The last time Frankolin and Felicia saw Scott, he had tacked a note on his front door.

I've started collecting dogs and revealing secrets. Dogs don't keep secrets like people do.

No love,
Your former son

SECRET MISSION

"Little dog, I can use you today," said Scott.

Little Sally bristled. She didn't like being called "little dog," but since the secret-catching pickup truck driver didn't know her real name, she'd have to put up with it.

After sampling enough high-quality dog treats—not your typical supermarket kind of treat but the fresh baked treats that true dog lovers give to dogs—little Sally started to think the secret catcher wasn't so bad after all. Maybe she'd let him look at her tag. What could it hurt? Then at least he could call her Sally. He didn't seem so bad. His treats tasted excellent. They even smelled good. Sometimes good treats have a bad odor, but not these treats. And she had never met a real-life secret catcher before. She knew lots of ball catchers, Frisbee catchers, and stick catchers, but not a secret catcher.

Scott leaned over to pick up little Sally. She

quickly calculated her options and decided to let him. He held her close to his face and looked her straight in the eyes and said, "You can help me catch a big secret today, if you don't mind."

No, I really don't mind, thought little Sally. *I think I'd like to help him. If he needs me, I shouldn't deny him. After all, that would be selfish, and one shouldn't be selfish in the face of important secret-catching work. I might be able to do some good. Maybe secrets shouldn't be kept. Maybe secrets are better told. Maybe the world would be filled with more Chihuahuas if there were fewer secrets.*

Little Sally puffed out her tiny chest as she thought about becoming assistant secret catcher. Her new position came with a lot of responsibility, but she knew a lot about responsibility. She had never lost a toy or abandoned a bone. Small dogs sometimes messed in the house, but not little Sally. She was too responsible for that.

Scott scratched behind her ears and said, "I've been working on breaking a big secret for a long time. When I saw you, I figured out how to do it. But I'll need your help. You're the smallest dog I know, and I bet only a very smart and very small dog can help catch this secret. I hope you can understand me."

Yes, thought little Sally, *I am smart and small. I can help catch a secret. Maybe I'll even save a life. Big dogs always get to save lives. When was the last time the news ran a story about a Chihuahua finding a lost mountain climber or saving a drowning boy? I can be that Chihuahua. I can catch secrets and save lives. I am Super Sally!*

"Woof," barked little Sally. She looked at his eyeballs. What did he have in mind? What was he planning on doing with her? How would she be helpful to a secret catcher? Scott stroked her back and then put his fingers under her ruby red collar and looked at her tag for the first time.

"Sally. What a pretty name for a little dog."

Big Sally growled. Scott looked over at her and said, "And what a pretty name for a big dog too. Okay, Sallys, here's the plan . . ."

43

THE PLAN

Here's what you need to know before you hear the plan.

On a dairy farm less than a mile from Compromise Road lived a cranky dairy farmer. No one knew if the dairy farmer was cranky because his milk smelled bad or if his milk smelled bad because he was cranky. The milk didn't exactly smell like crankiness, because crankiness doesn't really have a scent. His milk smelled more like skunk mixed with vinegar, which isn't an ideal smell for milk. It was also odd that a dairy that is located in a town without any skunks would produce milk that smelled like skunk mixed with vinegar. The townspeople stopped buying the cranky dairy farmer's milk because whenever their children drank it, they'd say things like "Yuck," "Ick," and "I think I'm gonna vomit." This made the cranky dairy farmer even crankier. In fact, he got

so cranky he started plotting his revenge.

"Soon they'll know what smelly really is," he told his cows. "I'll give them something to really say 'Ick' about," he'd say with a smile before realizing that a cranky dairy farmer should never smile, lest it take away some of his crank.

Now that you know that, we can move forward with the plan, except for one more thing you should know.

Scott had heard about the cranky farmer's threats, and since Scott had a sixth sense for secrets, he had a pretty good feeling the farmer was keeping one smelly-size secret. He had no idea what that secret could be, however, and couldn't figure out a way to infiltrate the farmer's property to find out.

He'd thought so much about uncovering this most top secret of secrets that he'd scratched a small hole in the side of his head trying to come up with a plan. He had a way with secrets, but some secrets were more top secret than others, and some secrets would always remain secret, no matter how hard a secret catcher tried to release them into the world.

When Scott had first seen little Sally, it was as if she had come to him bearing a plan. After taking one look at her, all his thinking and figuring seemed futile. A plan emerged, as if it had always been sitting there, just waiting to be picked up. All he needed was for the little dog to cooperate.

That is what you need to know. Now that you know everything you need to know, you can know the plan:

THE PLAN

Step 1: Go to Farmer Green's Famous
             Dairy Farm

Step 2: Put Sally in pocket

Step 3: Ask for milk

Step 4: When Farmer Green goes to get
             the milk, place Sally on the ground

Step 5: Distract Farmer Green

Step 6: Sally finds secret and comes back
             barking

Step 7: Sally leads me to the secret

The secret catcher picked up little Sally and held her close to his face. "Do you understand what to do?"

Sally wagged her tail.

"All right. Let's go."

44

FARMER GREEN

You WON't find GREEN EGGS at Farmer Green's FAMOUS DAIRY FARM
MilK ONLY!!!

The secret catcher and the Sallys drove down a short dirt road to Farmer Green's farm. Before they got out of the truck, little Sally cleared her throat with a few barks. Then she snuggled into the secret catcher's pocket and rolled herself up like a snail. She tried to make herself completely undetectable. If she could have flattened herself out, she would have.

"We'll be back soon," said the secret catcher to big Sally.

Big Sally wanted to help too. Sometimes being a big dog got in the way. She wasn't good at sneaking, and you had to be good at sneaking around to catch a secret. Big Sally wished there were something she could do to help.

With little Sally in his pocket, Scott got out of the truck and walked into a dilapidated wooden barn.

"I'd like to buy two quarts of milk."

A surprisingly handsome man with blond hair muttered a few foul words in reply. You'd never think someone so cranky could look so handsome, but this cranky farmer looked more like a movie star than a cranky farmer. Most cranky farmers look more like this:

"I'm busy. Go away. Why are you here?"

"For milk," repeated Scott.

"No one buys my milk," bellowed the farmer. "No one cares about dairy farmers, and I don't care about no one. They'll learn to care, though." Farmer Green turned around and stomped away.

Scott reached into his jacket pocket, lifted out little Sally, and gently placed her on the barn's dirt floor. Little Sally scurried away. Chihuahua legs never moved so fast. She hightailed it to the back of the barn. Farmer Green didn't notice her. If he had, he'd probably have thought she was just a barn rat anyway. Little Sally wondered what color this secret would be. Would it be green and shaped like a mean old affenpinscher? Or silver and pink and shaped perfectly, like a Chihuahua?

Little Sally saw two rusty trucks parked in a large field. She climbed over a woodpile and squeezed under a fence and looked at cows nuzzled up against more cows. Nothing looked or sounded too unusual. It's no secret that cows live on dairy farms. She squeezed back under the fence again and headed around to the other side of the barn.

"I wonder what that is," she said to herself. She scurried down to a zigzaggy wire fence. Her finely tuned nose picked up the oddest scent she'd ever smelled. She followed her nose even though the smell repulsed her and she felt like gagging, or even worse.

Moments later little Sally uncovered the secret of a lifetime. Unfortunately, the secret of a lifetime came with the stench of a lifetime too.

THE STENCH

Little Sally raced back to the secret catcher and barked as loudly as she could.

Farmer Green turned around and glared. "Hey, what's going on here?"

"What's that stench?" asked the secret catcher.

Little Sally barked. She felt woozy and didn't know how long she could keep barking. Her legs wobbled, and everything—the secret catcher, the farmer, and the farm—looked blurry. A foul odor filled the air. The farmer sounded even crankier than before. "I told you already. Get out! Go! Scat!"

He reached down and picked up a wooden baseball bat. "Maybe this will help you understand the meaning of "Get out!'"

Farmer Green ambled out from behind the counter. He lifted the baseball bat in the air with one arm. His eyes turned into little black beads and his lips tightened into a teeny knot.

BARK BARK BARK BARK BARK

Bark   BARK!

"What's the smell?" demanded the secret catcher.

Little Sally gasped for air between barks. Each breath she took felt like it might be her last. Her throat hurt so much that she thought she had swallowed a porcupine. She wanted to show the secret catcher what she had found, but she didn't know if she had the strength. She stumbled toward the back of the barn. Scott followed her. The farmer followed him, and with the might of a major-league baseball player, he swung the bat at the secret catcher's head. Little Sally fell to the ground.

BARK   BARK BARK

46
SKUNKS

When she opened her eyes, she saw the farmer lying next to her.

He hollered into her ear.

"I've been attacked!

"Help me!

"Somebody!

"Help me."

Big Sally stood on top of him and tapped his left shoulder with her paw.

"Good girl, Sally," said Scott. "You've come to the rescue. Keep him down until we find out what he's up to."

Little Sally struggled to find her footing and led Scott toward the most rancid smell in the history of Oaks Bluff. Scott pulled his shirt up over his mouth as he closed in on a massive congregation of . . .

Skunks.

He gagged and gasped for air.

Big Sally stood firm on top of the farmer.

"Get this beast off of me," said the farmer, coughing.

Big Sally barked ferociously. In her entire life big Sally had never bitten anyone. She didn't want to bite the farmer but knew she might have to, and if she had ever been angry enough to bite someone, this was the time. She could bite him. She could do it. She barked and thought about what it might feel like to bite a person. Generally, she preferred to lick, but she'd never met a person as terrible as the cranky farmer.

"What are you doing with all these skunks?" asked the secret catcher.

"Breeding them. Now get the beast off of me."

"Tell me why and she'll get off."

"No! Get her off. You're trespassing. This is assault."

Big Sally snarled. She'd show him assault if he wanted assault.

"Tell me why you have all those skunks," the secret catcher repeated.

"Revenge."

"Revenge on who?"

"All of you. Get the beast off me."

"Sally, stay! What are you planning to do with the skunks?"

"Agh. It feels like a refrigerator fell on my back. Help me."

"I'll help you," said the secret catcher. "But first tell me your secret. What are you doing with the skunks?"

"Fine. I'm gonna release them in town one night when everyone's asleep. If I'm lucky, in the morning the children going to school will get skunked, the parents going to work will get skunked, and all the happy people of Oaks Bluff will smell like the stench of skunk. Their food will smell like skunk. Their coffee will smell like skunk. Their clothes will smell like skunk, and their beautiful flowers will smell like skunk. Then maybe they won't care that their milk smells like skunk. Now get the dog off me."

"Okay, Sally. Come."

Big Sally jumped off of the farmer, but first she gave him a few licks because she felt bad for standing on him for such a long time. The farmer slowly stood up. His bones creaked and cracked, and blood drizzled out of his nose.

Little Sally waddled to the front of the barn. Big Sally followed her.

THE STINKY SMELL
OF SUCCESS

Big Sally took a big whiff and said, "You smell terrible."

"I feel terrible."

"I didn't know someone could smell so bad. No offense."

"Offense taken. Okay, fine, I'll give it back. I feel too bad to hold on to offense today. I'll take a rain check."

"Thanks. So, what did you see?"

"Skunks, hundreds of them: big skunks, little skunks, medium skunks, medium-large skunks."

"Wow. What happened?"

"I was quietly sneaking around looking for anything that might look like a secret, and my nose picked up an odd scent, so I followed it. It took me to the back of the barn. I was looking at all the cows, following the strange scent, when I noticed an unusual fenced area. At first I thought it was filled with big black rats. I tiptoed closer. I wasn't scared, not one bit. I had a job to do. I am, after all, an assistant secret catcher. I peeked in, but before I knew it, my face was nuzzled up against the fattest, blackest furry thing you've ever seen. To tell the truth, it felt kind of good."

"You were face to chest?"

"He was tall. Huge. Round. Soft and vicious. He stepped back, lowered his head, looked straight into my beautiful brown eyes, and turned around. I think it all happened very quickly but it seemed like it took forever. His huge black tail swung into the air, and a horrible spray shot out of his behind onto my face."

"Are you okay? You look yellow."

"I think I might die. Small dogs aren't supposed to get skunked. Getting skunked is for big dogs. Small dogs don't handle getting skunked too well. I think it can kill us."

"You think big dogs like getting skunked?"

"Sure. Why would they go out and get skunked all the time if they didn't like it? Don't you care that I might die?"

"You really have no idea what it's like to be a big dog. We're just like you only bigger, so we can run faster and farther. Sure our barks are lower-pitched, and we're more fun to play with, but we're still dogs."

"I'm going to die. Don't you care?"

"Sure I care. Come here."

Little Sally walked over to big Sally and collapsed onto her right paw.

"You really stink. I think I'll go care from over there," said big Sally.

"Die. I might die," howled little Sally.

"Hmmmmm," said big Sally. "I've never heard of a dog dying from getting skunked."

"I can't believe it. I'm going to be the first dog to die from skunk spray. Why me?" Little Sally gasped for air.

48

SKUNKS ON THE LOOSE

The secret catcher and Farmer Green stood eye to eye, smelly shirt to smelly shirt.

"Don't do it, Farmer Green. Don't punish the town. Let me help you figure out why your milk smells," pleaded Scott.

"What do you know about milk?"

"Nothing yet, but I know I can help you. Let me at least try. I own a bookstore. We have books about everything. I'm sure I can find out how to get the stink out of smelly milk."

The farmer wiped the blood from under his nose, looked across a field at several hundred grazing cows, and blurted out, "I don't want your help. Now get out of here.

Tell the town if you want, but I'm letting the skunks go and there's nothing you can do about it. Get out of here. Now."

The farmer limped over to the pen holding the skunks and fiddled with the latch. The more he fiddled, the more the skunks sprayed. He covered his nose and mouth with one hand and kept fiddling with the other.

"This isn't how I'd planned it, but this is how it's going to get done, and there's nothing you can do about it," bellowed Farmer Green.

"Wait. Stop. Can't we talk?"

"Talking isn't for me. I have nothing to say to you or anybody else." He lifted the latch and opened the gate. Skunks scattered across the farm and into the woods. Some sprayed as they passed by. Others simply passed by without much notice.

"Smell you later." Farmer Green laughed as he limped into the barn.

49

REUNITED

Frankolin and the Puddles drove down Compromise Road. They veered left and swung back to the right. They passed three houses on each side of the road before arriving at Scott's house.

Frankolin inhaled and looked at his throbbing finger. The king jumped about excitedly. Frankolin and the Puddles got out of the car and walked to the house. Frankolin knocked several times on the front door. No one answered. The sound of dogs barking spilled out. Baby peered in through a window. She saw big dogs, little dogs, medium dogs, and a dog with three legs. She didn't see a huge Great Dane or a tiny Chihuahua, however.

The cutest dog she saw looked like this:

Draw the cutest dog you can here:

"They're not in there," squeaked Baby. Her voice trembled, but she refused to cry.

The king couldn't echo Baby's restraint. He let out a pained whine. Tom looked at the king and started to whimper.

"I guess he's wrong," said Frankolin. "The king doesn't usually err. There must be something in the air."

The Puddles piled back into Frankolin's car. His finger throbbed as they drove up Compromise Road.

Halfway up the road, give or take, they passed a blue pickup truck.

"That's Sally!" yelled Baby. "Did you see that? That was big Sally's head sticking out the window."

"That was my son," said Frankolin.

"Turn around. Turn around. Turn around," yelled Baby.

"Calm down, Emily," said Mrs. Puddle.

Frankolin pulled a U-ey and sped back down Compromise Road.

"Can you drive faster?" begged Baby.

"Yeah," said Tom. "That dog looked like big Sally."

"It didn't look like big Sally. It was big Sally," insisted Baby.

They pulled up to the same house they had just left behind minutes before.

Baby bolted out of the car. Little Sally saw her first. Forgetting how terrible she felt, her tail took off in a fast and desperate wag. She ran to Baby and jumped up as high as she could. Baby picked her up and gave her a million kisses, even though she smelled awful. Big Sally licked Tom's face. Frankolin and Mr. and Mrs. Puddle walked over to Scott. Frankolin said, "These are friends of mine. They lost their dogs. I'm sorry to bother you, Son."

Mrs. Puddle stared at Scott. He looked familiar. More than familiar. It was as if she were looking in a mirror but a boy looked back. He had her round blue eyes, her freckled nose, and her heart-shaped

mouth. They even shared the same dimple on their
left cheek. He smelled worse than she did, though.

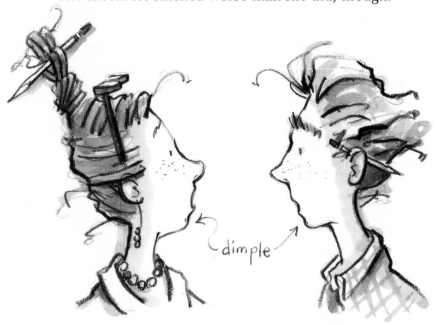

dimple

"Hmm. Weird," said Mrs. Puddle.

"It's nice to meet you," said Scott.

"Are you—," they both started at the same time.

"Oh, sorry. You first," said Scott.

"No, you go first. It's just that, well, you look so
familiar. You look like you could be family."

"Maybe I am," Scott said, and gulped.

"Scott," said Mrs. Puddle. "Is it possible? No,
never mind. It's nothing."

Scott turned to Frankolin. "Dad, is it possible?" he asked.

Frankolin's body tingled from his toes to his nose. Even his throbbing finger stopped throbbing and started tingling. "Dad, is it possible?" were the first words his son had said to him in twenty years. They were beautiful words, extraordinary words. Words to be memorialized and memorized.

"I'd like to introduce you to Pam Puddle. She's a part of the dancing Puddles and she's lost her dogs. I suppose and propose that if her parents happened to be named Claire and Abraham George Sheftoon, and if they ever put a son up for adoption about thirty-eight years ago, then the possibility is a probability that she's also your sister."

Mrs. Puddle figured the world could hear her heart belting out the most fantastic beat. After all these years of wondering, she stood face-to-face, freckle to freckle, with her brother. He didn't look like a baseball player with a mustache swinging off one side of his face, and he couldn't sit in the palm of her hand. No, he looked just like her.

"Indeed," she said. "You are my brother."

Scott, a.k.a. the secret catcher, a.k.a. Mrs.

Puddle's brother, walked over to his long-lost sister and swung his arms around her. Mr. Puddle threw his arms around the two of them. Baby stretched her arms around as many of them as she could. Tom joined the hug. Frankolin appeared taller. He hugged the huggers and said, "Scott, if you can hear me in there, I'd like to say, I'm sorry for the secrets. We did what we thought was best. It turned out to be worst. Sometimes I get confused."

From inside the hug, Scott replied, "I forgive you. I've missed you."

Frankolin's smile stretched along the width of his face. The Puddles got their dogs back. Frankolin got his son back. And Mrs. Puddle got her brother.

"Let's celebrate," said Frankolin. "We need to tell Felicia. We need to tell the world. Everything seems so clear. I'm not confused."

The huggers cheered.

"Get into the car. We're going home!"

The huggers cheered again.

Mr. Puddle, Mrs. Puddle, Scott, Frankolin, Baby, Tom, and the king got into Frankolin's car. Somehow everyone fit comfortably.

They drove down Compromise Road under a skunk-shaped cloud.

50

NOT AGAIN!

"They'll be back," said big Sally.

"I wonder," replied little Sally.

The two Sallys lay down next to each other and kept their eyes on the road.

THE END

or,

as Mrs. Puddle might say,

"The e-n-d. Period."

ABOUT THE AUTHOR AND ILLUSTRATOR

KATE FEIFFER is a writer, a filmmaker, a mother, and the author of four picture books for children, including *Double Pink*, illustrated by Bruce Ingman, which the *New York Times Book Review* praised for its "economy of style and understated wit," and *President Pennybaker*, illustrated by Diane Goode, which *Kirkus Reviews* called "breezy and charming and pleasingly subversive." Ms. Feiffer lives with her family on Martha's Vineyard, Massachusetts.

TRICIA TUSA is the beloved illustrator of many books for children, including the ALA Notable Children's Book *Fred Stays with Me!* by Nancy Coffelt.